"We pretend to be in love, we go to a dance, the money gets donated to the club and everyone is happy."

Lana laughed. "We'll both be miserable, and I don't think you could handle me for that long."

"You think I can't handle you?"

When he reached his arm out to stretch it across the back of her seat as he leaned in, Lana's breath caught in her throat. Agreeing to this engagement would mean the circumstances would be out of her control...but only temporarily.

"I see your mind working," Carson murmured. "Thirty days, Lana. That's all we need to make this ruse work for everyone."

Why did that husky, gravelly tone make her nerve endings stand at attention? And why did she suddenly have the urge to see if those lips were as soft as they looked?

* * *

From Feuding to Falling
by Jules Bennett is part of the
Texas Cattleman's Club: Fathers and Sons series.

Dear Reader,

Welcome to my installment with the Texas Cattleman's Club. I won't lie, I squealed a little when I saw the outline for this book. Enemies to lovers, a century-old secret and a fake engagement? Sign me up!

Carson and Lana are two headstrong individuals who are dynamic in their own unique ways. But just wait until they come together with their faux relationship to fool the town and the families that have been fighting for decades. What better way to end that than to join forces? Literally.

This couple was beyond fun to write. I hope you all love this powerhouse duo as much as I do. The Cattleman's Club is always a great place to visit. So, prop your feet up, grab your favorite drink and start turning those pages... Carson and Lana are waiting for you.

Happy reading,

Jules

JULES BENNETT

FROM FEUDING TO FALLING

HARLEQUIN

DESIRE

Special thanks and acknowledgment are given to Jules Bennett for her contribution to the Texas Cattleman's Club: Fathers and Sons miniseries.

DESIRE™

Recycling programs for this product may not exist in your area.

ISBN-13: 978-1-335-73541-6

From Feuding to Falling

Copyright © 2022 by Harlequin Books S.A.

This edition published by arrangement with Harlequin Books S.A.

For questions and comments about the quality of this book, please contact us at CustomerService@Harlequin.com.

Harlequin Enterprises ULC
22 Adelaide St. West, 41st Floor
Toronto, Ontario M5H 4E3, Canada
www.Harlequin.com

Printed in U.S.A.

USA TODAY bestselling author Jules Bennett has published over sixty books and never tires of writing happy endings. Writing strong heroines and alpha heroes is Jules's favorite way to spend her workdays. Jules hosts weekly contests on her Facebook fan page and loves chatting with readers on Twitter, Facebook and via email through her website. Stay up-to-date by signing up for her newsletter at julesbennett.com.

Books by Jules Bennett

Harlequin Desire

The Rancher's Heirs

Twin Secrets
Claimed by the Rancher
Taming the Texan
A Texan for Christmas

Lockwood Lightning

An Unexpected Scandal
Scandalous Reunion
Scandalous Engagement

Dynasties: Beaumont Bay

Twin Games in Music City
Fake Engagement, Nashville Style

Texas Cattleman's Club: Fathers and Sons

From Feuding to Falling

Visit her Author Profile page at Harlequin.com, or julesbennett.com, for more titles.

You can also find Jules Bennett on Facebook, along with other Harlequin Desire authors, at Facebook.com/harlequindesireauthors!

To all of the loyal readers who anxiously await my stories. Thank you for letting me fulfill a childhood dream and enjoy a career of making up stories.

One

"How's the new title, Mr. President?"

"Presidency looks damn good on me."

Carson Wentworth adjusted his tie in the mirror of his new plush office in the Texas Cattleman's Club clubhouse. His seventeen-year-old stepbrother, Tate, had called to check in as he usually did most mornings. They had a close bond and Carson knew Tate was proud of this accomplishment.

Tate had stood by his side the entire time from the start of the campaign. Their father had been around as well, but nobody supported Carson like his little brother.

"Do you often talk to yourself in the mirror?"

Carson jerked his attention away from the mirror and his cell on the table, focusing on his unexpected guest.

His rival, his enemy and the woman he couldn't get out of his damn fantasies. The very shapely, very intriguing Lana Langley was standing there giving him a once-over.

And it was that hoity-toity stare of hers that had him wanting to see if he could pull some kind of emotion out of her. He wondered if he peeled her from those body-hugging dresses and suits she wore, if she'd show him anything other than disdain.

"I'll call you later, Tate."

Carson tapped the cell to end the call without moving his gaze from Lana. The Langleys might be the sworn enemies of the Wentworths, but that memo had never quite reached his hormones.

Their families had started fighting a century ago, and from generation to generation, that animosity had been instilled in the children. But Carson's frustration with Lana had nothing to do with their families' past and everything to do with the fact she always seemed to be in his way.

She was too bold, too over-the-top. She had a take-charge attitude and he could appreciate that in some aspects of life, but they continually butted heads over what was best for the club.

Over the years, even a casual conversation would turn into something heated.

The damn woman was infuriating most days, but

those curves begged for a visual lick and he was all too willing to sample.

She had to know she drove men out of their minds with the way she dressed—like she'd just stepped off a magazine shoot for sexiest woman alive. Lana had a confidence and an audacious attitude that most found intimidating, but Carson saw her as a challenge…and he never backed down from a challenge.

"Giving yourself a little ego boost?" she asked, crossing her arms over her chest. "Staring at your reflection is a tad cocky, don't you think?"

"Confidence is an attractive trait," he retorted.

Her red lips spread into a slow smile. "Then you must think I'm sexy as hell."

Confident and sexy—yes. Those two terms definitely applied to Lana, but she wasn't just a family enemy, she'd also been his opponent in the TCC presidential race. She'd been quite a formidable opponent to beat, what with her being the chair of the Cattleman's Club Women's Association and all. Carson had defeated her by a good margin and come out on top, despite her having the backing of every female rancher around.

"Did you come to see my new office or did you need to discuss club business?" he asked, turning fully to face her. "I have a meeting in a few minutes, but I can spare a moment for you."

"Well, aren't I the lucky one," she muttered.

Her dry comment had him chuckling. Lana was

known for her quick wit, her independence, and for getting what she wanted...mostly. No doubt the recent loss still left a sting, but someone had to come in second and Carson never allowed himself to be vulnerable enough for anything less than number one.

"So what brings you here?" he asked.

Lana slowly crossed the open office area, her high heels echoing off the new hardwood floors. Carson watched as she examined the space, taking in the rustic decor of the sconces on the walls, which held photos of prior TCC presidents. Then she stopped when she got to his oversize mahogany desk. It was a piece he had brought in himself. He liked a large work space and wanted something of his own in this new role he'd taken on.

The silence made him twitchy...or perhaps those twitches came from watching her body shift beneath that sexy pencil dress in siren red. He couldn't tell if she'd come here to make him suffer or if she was taking in all she'd lost.

Perhaps a fair bit of both.

Finally, she turned to face him and laced her fingers in front of her body. The woman put up a good front of not giving a damn. She had her business face on and everything in Carson wanted to peel back that layer and see exactly what was beneath that steely exterior.

Passion...no doubt. A woman didn't dress with the confidence and sex appeal of Lana Langley and not have a burning passion beneath.

"Listen, Twenty-Two. My first order as club president was going to be focused on a new area exclusively for women," she began. "The good ol' boys ran this space for so long, and since women were allowed to become members ten years ago, we haven't our own designated space. That's too damn long to have to wait while we watch everything else get a face-lift around here. Everything in this building screams masculine and rustic, nothing is feminine. The ladies need something posh, something where we can unwind for a fun girls' night out."

Carson listened to her argument for changes at the club and realized she'd stopped. He'd heard it all before during the campaign and he didn't discredit her wants and needs. They just weren't going to be a priority on his current agenda, since he had a budget to stick to.

Silence continued to weigh heavy between them and her wide eyes were still locked solely on him. Clearly, she was waiting on his reply. He really didn't want to get into all of this when he was waiting on another woman to come through that door.

"Are you asking me a question or just telling me about your dashed dreams?" he queried.

Those bright blue eyes narrowed. "My dreams are far from dashed, Carson. I've given you time to settle in. Now I'm here as the chair of the women's association to make sure our needs are being met and we are getting what is fair and right. Just because I didn't win, doesn't mean I can't still fight for what we deserve."

Were they really going to have a showdown this early? He'd only had one cup of coffee and skipped breakfast. He needed more caffeine to deal with any type of altercation with Lana Langley. The woman was the most challenging person he'd ever dealt with. He could admit now that there had been a moment during the campaign he'd been worried she was going to win. She was damn good…but it wasn't something he'd admit to her.

The club meant too much to him, to his family. No matter the ties Lana had to the place, and hers were deep as well, but Carson had poured his entire heart into winning.

Carson actually did have a job to do within his family's ranching and oil business. The club was his escape, his joy. This was where he came to decompress…not negotiate with his sexy rival. The campaign had worn him out. He'd never worked harder in his life. Lana had challenged him at every turn and managed snappy, efficient comebacks when he would address a topic. If he hadn't been running, he would have voted for her. Again, not something he was about to admit to her.

Dealing with Lana was a necessity—Carson knew that. With their powerful positions here at the club, dealing with one another was inevitable. That didn't stop him from wishing they could just do phone calls or something else, rather than face-to-face meeting, where he had to take in the entire delectable package.

"While I appreciate your stance, what you're proposing sounds costly and there's no reason to—"

"There is every reason, Twenty-Two."

Carson shook his head. "Why do you keep calling me that?"

"If you'd done your homework on the club, you would know you're the twenty-second president."

"I'm well aware of the number I am." Carson sighed, really wishing he'd grabbed a second cup of coffee before that call with Tate. Maybe adding a little whiskey would've been a good idea as well. "Listen, I have an appointment any minute, so you're going to have to harass me another day."

That low, sultry laughter of hers filled the room, wrapping him in something too akin to arousal and he didn't like it. Not one bit. She made him so irritable and turned on, he'd instantly transformed into some kind of jerk with his words. He didn't mean to come across as condescending, but he'd opened his mouth and there it was.

Why this woman? Why couldn't someone, not a Langley, have him in knots? The media and locals had all been on the edge of their seats seeing how the feuding families would act during the campaign. Carson half wondered if they were waiting for the two of them to exchange punches or something. But there had been an agreement between the two of them going in. They weren't going to discuss their families' pasts because they each wanted to focus on the club and the future.

So at least that had been off the table.

"I've drawn up a proposal for the new women's area, along with a budget and bids from local contractors," she went on as if he hadn't said a word. "I actually emailed the options in very detailed spreadsheets to you this morning, so they will be in your inbox now. Once you go over that, we can discuss moving forward."

Wow. She really was something. The way she attempted to steamroll right over him took guts, but he wasn't having it. The rivalry between the Wentworths and the Langleys went back a century and didn't appear to be ending anytime soon.

Carson could see that if he didn't nip this in the bud now, she would become an issue now that he was president, and she'd try to see just how far she could push her own authority.

Perhaps her loss had damaged her pride more than he thought, or maybe she was one of those people who refused to admit defeat. Either way, he was in charge of the club, including any renovations and budget, and she needed to recognize that.

While Carson admired and even found Lana's determination attractive, he also knew if she even thought for a second that she could wrap him around her finger…she damn well would.

"There will be no moving forward," he informed her, taking a step closer. "I have other projects that need my immediate attention and building on an entire new wing isn't in the funds right now. I will take a look at this project for the future, but it certainly isn't on the top of my list right now."

Those blue eyes turned icy as she continued to hold his gaze. The woman was relentless, not backing down from something she wanted. Good for her. He admired her tenacity, but that didn't mean he'd give in, nor did he want to. Maybe it was about time Lana learned the word *no*.

"You'll see it is in the budget when you look at the proposals I sent over," she stated through gritted teeth. "I'm not sure why you aren't even up to discussing this unless you're afraid of—"

"I'm not afraid of anything where you're concerned."

Except this growing, unwanted, unnecessary attraction. Those damn curves got him. He loved nothing more than running his hands over the slopes and silky skin of a shapely woman. And, damn it, Lana was lusciously shaped in exactly all of his favorite spots. Too bad she was a Langley.

"Excuse me?"

Carson turned toward his open doorway to see Sierra Morgan standing there with a smile on her face. The investigative journalist who had come to town a few months ago to do a piece on the Texas Cattleman's Club's tenth anniversary of admitting women members had ended up staying longer, as she'd decided to write a book on the subject and then stumbled upon even bigger stories.

Now, freelancing for the *Royal Gazette*, she not only was investigating a historical feud involving club members that would connect to her book, but she was also writing stories about an abandoned baby found in the hospital parking lot back in October...and the continuing search for the baby's father, who was supposedly a TCC member. Sierra had found herself caught up in all the scandals and secrets Royal, Texas, had to offer.

Now she wanted to interview Carson about his new position as president, though he had a strong feeling this session would turn into a grilling about his great-grandfather. Harmon Wentworth thought he was near death, and he was determined to discover who his birth mother was before he passed on. In whatever spare time she had, Sierra seemed to be helping Harmon, using a diary filled with clues.

Carson resisted the urge to rake a hand over his head because he seriously needed to get that second cup of coffee before tackling this interview. There was too much drama, too many secrets floating around this town, and he didn't want any of that to overshadow one of the biggest accomplishments of his life.

"Is this a bad time?" Sierra asked.

"Yes," Lana replied.

"No," Carson said at the same time.

Sierra's smile faltered as her eyes darted between the two. "I can come back," she suggested as she started to turn back around.

"Not at all."

Carson refused to let Lana have any control, especially where club business was concerned. Again, the woman needed to learn who was in charge.

"We have an appointment and Lana was just leaving."

He focused his attention back on her and raised his eyebrows.

"I was?" she asked with a wide smile and a little lilt in her tone. "I thought we were just getting started on negotiations."

"Actually, since you're both here, maybe I could interview you, too, Lana?" Sierra asked.

Now Carson did rake a hand over the back of his neck and sighed. Great. Just what he wanted. He'd lost control to his enemy and a nosy reporter. So much for being president.

Damn it.

Things could only get better from here…right?

From Carson's tight lips and stiff posture, it seemed Mr. President wasn't thrilled one bit with the idea of her sticking around for this impromptu dual interview.

Lana couldn't help but smile, knowing full well she was getting under Carson's skin. Well, that was just too bad because he'd been under hers for too damn long.

Aside from the presidential race, where her loss left her ego too bruised for comfort, she found him far too attractive.

And why was that? The man was arrogant and egotistical, not to mention he was a Wentworth. Might as well be a spawn of the devil himself because the Wentworths and the Langleys meshed about as well as fire and ice, all because one hundred years ago there had been a lover's tryst and hidden secrets. None of that had anything to do with any of them today, but for whatever reasons, people just couldn't let the war die off.

Settling into the leather club chair across from Carson's oversize desk, Lana crossed her legs and flashed her smile to Carson as he took a seat and shot her a glare.

Poor baby. He was getting steamrolled by two powerful women. Must be hell on his overinflated ego.

He'd gotten a cup of coffee from the coffee bar in the corner after Sierra and Lana had both declined a cup. Now he looked like he wanted something a bit stronger in that mug.

"This is just great," Sierra said as she pulled her notebook and pen from her bag. She shifted her focus to Carson. "Before we get to how the new presidency is going and the future of the club, I'd love to get your take on your great-grandfather searching for information on his birth mother."

Lana perked up at that statement as she watched Carson's reaction. His eyebrows drew together and he eased forward in his seat, but before he could respond, Sierra went on.

"As you know, in addition to researching the Texas Cattleman's Club, I've been doing some articles on the abandoned baby, Micah. Just to catch you up… After finding his deceased mom's diary, we were able to connect Micah with his aunt Eve. Eve Martin had been heading to the hospital to look into DNA testing for Micah when she suddenly fell ill from a heart condition—the same genetic condition that killed her sister, Micah's mother, Arielle. Eve barely made it to the lobby before passing out. Now we know she left her nephew in his carrier on the trunk of a car—a car that belonged to your cousin, Cammie Wentworth. Cammie, along with her fiancé, Drake, are serving as the baby's foster parents until Eve can recover enough to resume custody.

"But the unknown father remains a mystery. And there were rumors all over town as to who he could be. I'm using Arielle's diary to find any suspects.

The diary says he's a club member—I'm still working on that—but the diary also has some interesting information in there about your great-grandfather Harmon and his search for his birth mother.

"Arielle was helping him with research before she died. I've decided to take over where she left off. Another mystery to solve," Sierra stated, pulling in a deep breath. "And there's also mention that Harmon wants the Wentworth-Langley feud to come to an end. He wants peace restored to the families in his lifetime, but no one knows what started the feud a century ago."

Lana marveled at how Sierra knew all of this, but the woman was a top investigative reporter, so she had her ways. She had come to town to do a piece on the history of the Texas Cattleman's Club, which had become a book project. Her timing couldn't have been better. She'd stumbled onto several town mysteries.

Now Sierra found herself all tangled up in the intricate weave of the web known as Royal, Texas.

Every single day seemed to bring some new nugget of information and Lana figured Sierra was having the most exciting career moment of her life.

"I've been following your stories about Micah. You're a good writer. But I'm not really at liberty to discuss my great-grandfather," Carson stated, clasping his hands together on his desk. "Our family issues are between us and certainly nothing I want in your reporting, since we all have mixed views on the quarreling between the Wentworths and the Langleys."

"Well, I do have the diary right now." She pulled the item from her purse and placed it on Carson's desk. "It was rather enlightening, but there are still chunks missing and that's what I need to find. I don't like missing puzzle pieces."

Sierra pursed her lips before turning to Lana. "And what about you? Do you have any input on this feud?"

Lana had always wondered what on earth could have been so bad that the hatred of two families could last for generations. What would be so terrible and unforgivable that it had to trickle down the lineage?

Lana had heard rumors of relationships gone wrong, but she really never asked questions. She'd been too busy living her own life in the here and now to worry about something petty that happened a century ago.

Still, just because she wanted to ignore it, didn't mean it didn't exist. But, because of the wedge between the families, Lana had never even tried to be chummy with Carson...and because of that arrogant personality of his, she was just fine with that.

"I can't give you any information on the family feud," Lana replied, honestly. "But I wouldn't mind visiting Harmon and finding out what he knows firsthand."

"Like hell."

Carson's outburst had both women jerking their attention toward him.

"And why is that?" Lana asked, straightening her spine. "Aren't you interested?"

"Ancient history is irrelevant to my life now," Carson stated.

"Actually, I've been wondering if Harmon's birth mother is what started this feud between the Langleys and the Wentworths." Sierra pursed her lips and tapped the tip of the pen against her notebook. "And a source told me Harmon said he wasn't going to release his fortune to the Texas Cattleman's Club upon his death if the two families are still at odds with each other."

Lana couldn't tear her gaze away from Carson. Clearly some of what Sierra had just shared wasn't news to him, but he seemed surprised that she had that information.

This town was riddled with secrets and it was giving Lana a headache. Lana really just wanted to focus on her own goals, which she'd set while she'd been campaigning. She'd wanted to continue the hard work her sister-in-law, Abby, had started ten years ago. Abby had fought to make the clubhouse coed and had been the first female club member. Abby had been Lana's biggest cheerleader and confidante during the presidential campaign. No doubt this loss had torn at Abby's heart just as much as Lana's.

But just because Lana had lost didn't mean she couldn't fulfill a need where she saw fit. The women of the club still needed an area they could call their own, something luxurious and extravagant that didn't scream of male ruggedness.

One thing at a time, though. Right now, she had to deal with Sierra, Carson, and the idea of seeing Harmon.

Making sure to keep her own questions to herself, Lana took in a good breath of self-control and waited on Carson to say something regarding Harmon.

"Whatever my great-grandfather has going on with his past or his fortune really isn't fodder for the press," Carson added. "But, if you want to talk about my new title here at the club, I would be more than happy to get into that conversation."

"I mean no disrespect," Sierra scoffed. "I'm simply an investigative journalist doing my job. Maybe Lana has an opinion on Harmon and these rumors."

Oh, Lana had opinions for sure, but she was smart enough to hold her thoughts inside…for now.

"Do you want to know what started this battle between the families?" Sierra urged.

"It's certainly something I've thought about over the years," Lana admitted. "But this has gone on for so long and really doesn't have anything to do with me, exactly. Generations are just trained from the start to know who they are at odds with. Sounds like Harmon is tired of the pettiness and wants to resolve things while he's still alive."

Lana pursed her lips, then spoke before she could think twice. "I'd love to pay Harmon a visit. I mean, I'm a Langley and if he really wants to put an end to this feud, perhaps we can work something out."

"Hell no."

This was the second time an outburst from Carson surprised her. She'd known he had a defiant opinion and could be outspoken, that much had been obvious during their election campaign, but she'd never seen him this defensive. Lana couldn't help but wonder what he was so worried about.

"And why is that?" Lana asked. "Maybe we can put this to rest once and for all, plus get those funds for the club. You already made a comment about my ideas and the budget. There's no reason I can't pay him a visit."

"Then I'm coming, too."

Judging from his wide eyes and slight intake of breath, apparently Carson was just as surprised by his abrupt statement as Lana.

"Fine. I'll be back this afternoon and we can head over." She got to her feet and glanced to Sierra. "I do apologize, but I have to run. Maybe we can do lunch or coffee sometime and you can interview me."

Sierra nodded with a bright smile. "I'd love that."

Lana didn't bother saying goodbye to Carson as she made her way out of his office. She had a few errands to run and she wanted to change her clothes. She'd put on a killer outfit for this morning's verbal sparring session with Carson, but to pay a visit to Harmon in the assisted-living facility, she wanted to be a little more comfortable and conservative.

That's not to say she still couldn't have a killer outfit, though. She had curves—curves that she actually loved accentuating and showing off. And it wasn't lost on her that Carson seemed to appreciate a shapely woman as well. For years she'd been aware of him visually sampling her, and though he might despise her, simply for her name if no other reason, she knew that he found her attractive. She'd have to be completely oblivious to not notice…and Lana was quite aware of everything about Carson Wentworth. From his sexy Southern drawl to his broad, muscular frame.

Too bad he was a Wentworth and she was a Langley.

Two

As if her body-hugging dress from this morning wasn't enough, now Lana was wearing ass-hugging jeans, a red sweater, and cowgirl boots. Carson stood at her front door taking in the total package and wishing he would have really thought this through. He needed to keep his distance, but since she'd insisted on seeing Harmon, Carson would damn well be going with her.

Lana looked totally different than she had earlier in his office. She'd pulled up her long, dark hair into a high ponytail and looked too damn adorable, like the girl next door...but he knew the vixen that she truly was.

Lana could go from CEO style to country girl in

a snap and both looks were hell on Carson's system. He shouldn't want to find her attractive, but damn it. She'd been a stunner all through school, and the older they got, the sexier she became. That body nearly had him forgetting he'd been conditioned his entire life to despise her and anyone else with that dreaded last name.

The shape of Lana Langley could make any man forget everything else, except the hope of exploring…

Stop. Just stop. Carson had to get control over his thoughts or he'd look like a damn fool. She knew what she looked like and that was likely why she purposely tried to drive him out of his ever-loving mind with want and need. She was aiming to get those wily claws in him and if he didn't focus on his own life and his own goals, he'd fall prey to her.

Now that the election was over, Carson needed to shift back to finding the social life that he'd put on hold for so long. Go on a date, get laid, anything to exorcise Lana from his mind.

Getting entangled with a Langley wouldn't bode well for either of them. Not when the feud was front and center now, with Harmon's will conditions and that diary with his thoughts floating around. Thankfully, though, Sierra had gotten Eve's permission to lend him Arielle's diary to see if he could spot any clues Sierra had missed. Carson wished the family war had never started, then maybe he and Lana wouldn't already have this rift between them. He wouldn't mind exploring his attraction to her, if that was the case.

But that wasn't the reality he lived in—not only did the war exist, but the two of them had also thrust it into the limelight with their campaign, as the Wentworths and Langleys went at it again.

"What are you doing here?" she demanded, holding on to her front door.

Carson was starting to question that himself. Clearly he was a masochist, but he preferred to cling to the fact he would try to have the upper hand wherever and whenever possible. He hadn't gotten this far in his life by letting others get the edge over him.

"I'm here to take you to see my great-grandfather."

Lana rolled her eyes. "I told you we'd meet at your office, and I'm more than capable of driving myself."

"It's a free service from your new club president."

Now those piercing eyes narrowed. "I like the amenities the way they are, Twenty-Two."

"Quit calling me that," he commanded.

"It's a free service," she retorted.

Why? Why had he thought coming here and taking her was the smartest move he could make? Because clearly he should have met her at the office and merely monitored her there.

But he wanted to talk to her before they went in to see Harmon, and now he realized texting or a simple old-school phone call would have proved just as efficient. Yet, here he was on her porch, and leaving now would only make him look weak, which was the last thing he could afford around Lana.

"If we're riding together, I'm driving," she commented with a smirk. "I only relinquish control when absolutely necessary."

That naughty grin, combined with the bold statement, had him visualizing Lana spread out on his bed beneath him, thoroughly enjoying everything he gave…and not one bit in control, as she came utterly undone beneath his touch.

In that instant he knew he was in for trouble—just how much was the scariest part. And he also had to assume that whole control comment of hers was also a warning.

Their verbal sparring matches were continually ongoing. Different day, same banter laced with sexual tension. At some point, one of them was going to snap.

"Fine," he conceded. "I don't have trouble giving up control."

Lana stared into his eyes, then her gaze dropped to his mouth before she looked directly at him once again. "I do find that difficult to believe. Someone like you would never give up control."

Carson took a step forward before he even realized he'd moved. Suddenly, he was within an inch of her face and her swift intake of breath seemed to wrap around him. So, like the masochist he was, Carson took this a step further.

"A powerful, confident man knows when to let the lady take charge," he murmured, pleased when her eyes widened and that dainty pink tongue moistened her red lips. "There are many circumstances when I'm more than happy to let my woman dominate me."

Shut up. Shut up. Why the hell was he doing this? Why couldn't he get that image of Lana and her sweet curves wrapped in his sheets out of his mind? And why was he playing the mental game of foreplay? None of this made sense, but he couldn't stop himself. It was as if his mind had two completely different compartments and they were battling against each other: common sense versus aching desire.

Lana took a step back and tipped her chin. "Good thing I'm not your woman," she replied. "I'm positive you and I would never get along, no matter how sexy those seductive words and mental images are."

Carson said nothing, but remained in her doorway holding her gaze.

"You *were* trying to seduce me with your words, were you not?" she asked, quirking one dark, perfectly arched eyebrow.

Carson couldn't help but smile. "Are you looking to be seduced, Lana?"

Those striking blue eyes darted to his mouth

once more and hovered there a fraction longer than he was comfortable with.

Carson stepped onto the threshold and her focus came back up to his eyes. She said nothing, and he wondered if she wasn't a Langley and he wasn't a Wentworth what would happen if he closed that door behind him and flicked the lock. Would she welcome him in? Would she make good on the promise that stare had been offering up?

Mercy, they'd tear each other up in the bedroom. If he thought their encounters were heated now, he couldn't even imagine what might happen when he got her into his bed.

When? No, that couldn't be...could it? Why did he automatically assume they'd be intimate?

They were the modern-day Montagues and Capulets, and sex, no matter how amazing it would be, wouldn't change their names or circumstances. And, damn it, he knew they'd be combustible and it would likely be the greatest affair he'd ever enter into.

Carson nearly cursed himself. They hadn't entered into any agreement, sexual or otherwise, and he'd already somewhat dubbed her the best he'd ever had? Clearly, he needed to call one of his lady friends and remove Lana from the forefront of his mind.

"We need to leave." Her voice cracked a little, then she cleared her throat and reached for her purse, which was hanging by the door. "Step aside."

Carson stepped back outside, onto the porch and off to the side so she could come out. He needed to remember that command of staying out of her way because now that the election was over, there really was no need for them to worry about seeing each other as often. There were no debates, no TCC rallies or meet-and-greets. They'd run into each other at the clubhouse and maybe an occasional society affair, but nothing more than that.

Which might help him tamp down his attraction and ease his mental state. He'd likely go mad if he had to keep in too much contact with the intriguing, lush Lana Langley.

All of those verbal matches over the last few months had only made the great divide even larger...unfortunately, it had also made him realize just how sexy and powerful she truly was.

Lana walked beside Carson as they entered the assisted-living facility. On the ride over Carson had attempted to lecture her in the dos and don'ts of her visit with Harmon, but she'd completely tuned him out.

Honestly, how did he expect her to even form a coherent thought, let alone try to hold a conversation? She'd stared out the window for fear that her entire face, neck, and upper chest was flushed because of the way Carson had lowered his voice and made his Southern drawl all the more arousing.

And why was that? She'd grown up in Royal, so that sexy twang was all she'd heard her entire life. Why did this man and his toe-curling tone have to get to her?

At first, she'd only assumed because he was off-limits, but now…she honestly didn't know. During the debates, he'd gotten under her skin in all sorts of ways. He'd been demanding and cocky, and she'd found that both annoying and sexy as hell.

"Remember what I told you," Carson said as he turned to her.

Remember? If she'd heard the first time maybe that would be an option.

Lana pasted on a smile and nodded because she just wanted to get into this room to see what Harmon Wentworth would share about the epic family feud. At one hundred, the man certainly wasn't getting any younger and she really didn't want the secrets dying with him.

"Believe it or not, I don't make a habit of badgering the elderly. I save that for my opponents."

Lana patted his cheek, shocked when that coarse scruff on his jawline raked against her palm. Her entire body zinged from just that one, simple act and she couldn't help but wonder how that facial hair would feel against her bare skin in more…delectable areas.

Carson reached up and grabbed her hand before she could remove it. The muscle beneath her palm clenched and she couldn't tear her eyes away from his for anything. She should, though. She should jerk her hand away, turn and waltz into Harmon's room, yet she stood here staring at those captivating green eyes, wishing they were somewhere else more private.

No. She couldn't wish such naive things. Carson didn't like her any more than she liked him. Even in school they'd hung out with opposite crowds and kept their distance just because of the simple fact that she'd always been told to avoid the Wentworths. All those years of having that drilled into her head went right along with the opinion she'd formed on her own, that he was an arrogant man.

She could find Carson attractive, but there was no way in hell she could act on unwanted desire. He was just getting under her skin, that's all.

Before she could speak or move her hand away, the door was flung open. Carson jerked in surprise and Lana removed her hand from his face...but not before she caught the smile from the nurse and the curious look of Harmon, who was seated and had clearly seen the near embrace.

"So sorry," the nurse said as she stepped back. "Please, come on in. I was just passing Mr. Wentworth his afternoon medications."

Lana moved into the room and was surprised how spacious and homey the private suite appeared. For assisted living, this was rather nice. Though Harmon certainly had the money and wouldn't pay to just be anywhere. This room was likely the nicest in the entire place and seemed more of a posh hotel rather than a home for seniors who needed assistance.

Carson returned the smile to the nurse before heading in. Once the nurse stepped out, he closed the door behind him before turning back to his great-grandfather.

"Well, this is a nice surprise," Harmon stated.

The elderly man's wide grin sent deep wrinkles scrunching around his eyes and hairline. His silver hair had been combed neatly away from his face and he was wearing a button-up shirt and dress pants. He had on slippers and there wasn't a doubt in Lana's mind the man would much rather have on his cowboy boots.

Harmon Wentworth had been a staple in Royal for decades. The man could always be seen in the bar at the clubhouse and he'd been known for ruthless business transactions. He had been quite the mogul in his day.

But those days of farming and ranching and running his empire were over for Harmon. That was the brutal reality of life. Everything came to an end at some point whether you were ready or not.

"And who do you have here?" Harmon asked, using the arms of the chair to ease himself up.

He pasted on a smile and extended his hand like

the Southern gentleman he'd been raised to be. Lana crossed the room and immediately took his hand.

"I'm Lana Langley, Mr. Wentworth. It's so nice to meet you."

His grip was firm, but he quickly released her hand. Those white, bushy eyebrows rose as Harmon's attention shifted to Carson. Behind her, Carson moved toward them.

"Langley?" Harmon asked, clearly surprised. "Carson, I didn't certainly expect something this fantastic."

Lana watched as a slow smile turned into a low laugh and Harmon pulled Carson into an embrace before releasing him and reaching for her.

"This is wonderful news," he declared. "Simply wonderful. I never thought I'd see the day, but I'm so glad I'm still on this earth for this moment. I can honestly say, I don't know that I've had a happier moment in the last several years than this right here."

Lana nearly stumbled as he ended the hug, but she pulled herself together with a deep breath. What was he talking about?

Harmon gestured to the sofa across from his sitting chair. "Please, sit. Why didn't I hear about this relationship before now? Finally, a Langley-Wentworth union. I never thought I'd see the day."

"Sir—"

"So, how long have you two been together?"

Harmon asked, cutting off Lana as she took a seat next to Carson. "I hope this isn't just something temporary. A long-term commitment would simply be... Well, life-changing."

"A serious relationship with Lana," Carson chuckled. "Grandfather, she and I—"

"Are hopefully heading down the aisle soon," he said with a grin as he eased back into his chair. "This is absolutely epic, Carson. I wanted the families to bury the hatchet, so to speak, but I never thought an engagement would come from my warnings. No matter if this makes the family angry or not, it's time for this to end. I meant it when I said I would be withholding my funds from the clubhouse upon my death if there isn't some unification or rebuilding of the relationships between the Langleys and the Wentworths. But an engagement... I hope I'm not getting carried away. From what I saw in the doorway, you two are in a committed relationship, right?"

"Engaged?" Lana whispered, her gaze darting to Carson as her heart clenched in her chest.

In a moment that shocked her even more than opening her door to see Carson standing on the other side earlier, he reached for her hand and gave a squeeze. She didn't like that silent gesture and dread settled deep as she feared she'd just stepped into an impossible situation.

Absolutely not. This was not happening.

"We wanted to come here and tell you first," Carson said in a voice far too calm under these absurd circumstances. "I knew you would be happy with the news."

Lana kept her focus on Carson, silently willing him to glance her way so he could see what she was sure was her best death glare.

What the hell kind of game was this? Had this been a setup on his part? Is that why he'd insisted on accompanying her?

Well, she couldn't let this go on for one more minute. Faking an engagement or any other type of union with Carson was wrong. Not only was it wrong, but it was also never going to become a reality.

Lana started to step forward, but Carson's grip tightened for a fraction of a second. His eyes held hers now and she saw it—pleading. Never in her life had she seen such a gesture from Carson. If this had been some type of setup, he had a reason. And they were going to have one hell of a talk once they left because she deserved an explanation.

"So, when is the big day?" Harmon asked, his thick eyebrows raised and his dark eyes wide. Clearly, the man was eager for details.

Carson held her gaze another second before turning his attention back to his great-grandfather.

"Everything is still so new, we haven't made any arrangements," Carson replied.

Harmon nodded. "I suppose with the club presidential race and all of that, you two haven't had a chance to do much else."

"We haven't," Carson acknowledged. "We actually both had an interview this morning with Sierra Morgan. She's digging around into your past and the feud. That diary of Arielle Martin's has really piqued everyone's interest."

"That's one of the reasons I wanted to come see you, Mr. Wentworth," Lana chimed in, really needing to take back some semblance of control.

"Call me Harmon. You're joining the family."

Like hell.

"Can you tell us anything about why this feud started and why it's still going on?" Lana asked.

Harmon glanced out the window next to his chair and seemed to be contemplating how to answer, or even if he was going to give her a response. Lana slipped a side glance to Carson, whose eyes remained on his great-grandfather.

Coward. She never took Carson for a coward, but the man wasn't able to look at her. Well, he couldn't hide forever and he would certainly be getting an earful the moment they got to the parking lot.

Another bubble of fury started within her when she thought back to Carson at her home. He'd been flirty, almost too much. Was this why? Damn it. He had a plan and he hadn't wanted to tell her?

Did he think she'd actually go along with this

preposterous scheme? He might have won the TCC presidency over her, but there was no way he was taking charge here and forcing her hand into some engagement. Even if she was looking for a husband, Carson Wentworth would be the last one on the list.

No, he wouldn't even *be* on the list.

"I think the feud started with my birth, but I don't know anything else," he answered. "Now I want to find who my birth mother was before I die and I wanted this feud settled, so I guess I'm halfway there."

Harmon now seemed to believe that the families were merging together, and he was sitting there looking back at her with such happiness, she would only be a jerk if she called out Carson on his lie now.

"I'm not sure when we'll actually...marry." Lana couldn't believe she was even speaking these words. "We're both pretty busy people."

Harmon nodded. "I understand, Lana. No rush on the wedding. But what do you all say you have an engagement party at the club at the end of the month? We can celebrate your union and the end of the family feud. You can then make an announcement that I will be donating an exorbitant sum to the club for any renovations or new amenities you both deem necessary. You won't have to wait until I die to get the money."

Was she seriously considering this farce?

Yes, she was. Because if lying for a short time would finally end this century-old battle, then she didn't mind doing her part.

But, an entire month? That seemed so long. Weeks worth of pretending to be in love with Carson? What would that entail? Scenarios bounced around her mind, from holding hands to kissing to…

No. There could be nothing else. If they had to fake anything, it would all be in public for show. Nothing more.

Once this was all said and done, Lana would have the funds she'd wanted for the women's lounge. Abby would be proud that Lana was continuing the hard work she'd started a decade ago.

"How are you settling into your new role?" Harmon asked Carson.

Well, obviously the man had spoken and assumed they would just fall in line with his demands. How in the hell had her impromptu idea to visit only hours ago suddenly lock her into a month-long engagement to a man she hated…yet desired so much more than she should have? She didn't want to hurt Harmon, despite him being a Wentworth. The man had done nothing personal to her—he seemed genuine, and he just wanted to make peace. How could she go against that?

"I'm excited to get started on the new plans

and the next chapter," Carson replied as if his life hadn't just taken a drastic turn in the last five minutes.

Lana listened as Harmon and Carson discussed club business, clearly having moved beyond the engagement chat or anything regarding the diary.

And Carson still had a hold of her hand. Oh, she could pull away, but then what would that look like? Maybe there was some reason Carson wanted to enter into this absurdity. Maybe he wanted this so Harmon would give the club the donation. She couldn't deny that she wanted those funds, too, and clearly this was the price she'd have to pay.

Lana had so many questions and concerns assaulting her from all directions, and she didn't want to sit around here making small talk. She wanted to get back out into the privacy of her vehicle and make Carson explain himself.

The conversation between the two men seemed to go on and on. Lana tried to focus on what they were talking about, but nothing of any importance was said about the diary or the fighting that dated back a century. That had been the sole purpose of Lana's visit. Never in her life had she expected to be trapped in such a circumstance, where she saw no immediate way out.

And the longer she sat here, pretending like nothing was wrong, like her life hadn't just come to a halt, the angrier she became.

She'd grown up surrounded by lies and deceit. Her mother had put up with that for far too long and Lana vowed never to be weak or a pushover when it came to men. Her father had been so dishonest about every aspect of his life and Lana's mother had simply gone right along with it, never questioning.

Lana found out years later about the affairs and the financial troubles her parents were having. While her mother continued to always put up a perfect front, Lana's father continued to live his filthy, lying life of infidelity.

Finally, Lana got to her feet and smiled at Harmon. "You'll have to excuse us, Mr. Wentworth."

"Harmon, remember?" he reminded her. "We're going to be family."

Lana nodded her head and offered, "Harmon. I'm sorry, but I do have an appointment with my sister-in-law shortly and we'll have to be going."

"Oh, I'm terribly sorry for droning on and on," he stated, as he slowly pushed to his feet and steadied himself on the arms of the chair. "Keep me updated on the engagement party and the wedding date. It was wonderful to see you, Carson."

Harmon turned to Lana and extended his hand once again. "And you, too, young lady. I look forward to hearing more about this union."

That made two of them, because this was just as new to her as it was to him.

"Nothing will bring me greater joy than seeing this feud finally put to rest." Harmon smiled and shook his head. "I never dreamed a wedding would turn these families around. Once and for all we will be joined in love instead of divided by hate."

Lana saw her opening and dove in headfirst.

"I hope I'm not overstepping here, but since I will be—" she swallowed the lump "—joining the Wentworth family, what started all of this fighting?"

"I don't remember. It was so long ago..." Harmon's eyes seemed to dim as his lids lowered. "Along with the feud, my birth mother is still a mystery. I'd do anything to have that truth uncovered. When Arielle came through doing research, I told her everything I know."

Lana felt for him. She really did. His time on this earth was running out and he just wanted answers. He not only wanted answers, but he also wanted all of this hatred put to rest once and for all.

But this trouble that started so long ago wasn't her fault, had nothing to do with her whatsoever, actually. So she shouldn't have to be punished... should she?

"I'll come by later in the week to see you," Carson promised.

The two men embraced and something flipped in Lana's chest. She hadn't imagined Carson as much of a family man. She knew he was close to his stepbrother, Tate, but other than that, she didn't bother herself thinking of anything else regarding his personal life.

She'd known him since grade school, but he'd been an arrogant brat back then, playing all the sports, being the jock, and dating all the "perfect" girls with their teased hair and itty-bitty figures.

Her opinion of him hadn't changed much over the years. He still came off as an arrogant jerk... like when she'd found him admiring himself in the mirror earlier while on speakerphone.

But there was something about seeing him softer with Harmon that made her wonder if there was another side to Carson and why he never let the public see that one. Why was he always so harsh, so controlled, and powerful? Maybe he did have actual human feelings beneath that steely exterior.

Not that she wanted to see him in any other manner. She needed that arrogance, that stiff upper lip he had, because if he rid himself of either of those qualities, she'd be in trouble. That sex appeal could only be ignored for so long and she'd done a damn good job in her all of her thirty-two years.

But she wasn't about to let this little stunt go.

As she marched ahead of him to the car, Lana already had her virtual bullet-point presentation in her head regarding all the questions she needed answers to.

Sexy or not, there was no way in hell she was going to pretend to be okay being engaged—fake or otherwise—to Carson Wentworth.

Three

He'd barely gotten his door closed before Lana laid into him. She'd tossed him her keys in the parking lot, a definite warning she was pissed.

"You are out of your ever-lovin' mind if you think I'm going to act like the doting fiancée."

The fact that she gave up the driver's seat for the ride back was not a good sign.

He raked a hand down his face and blew out a sigh before shifting in his seat and turning to focus on her. Oh, she was angry. Those expressive eyes were wide, unblinking, and her lips had thinned. He didn't have to know her strong personality to figure out she'd not been too thrilled inside at the bomb that had been dropped between them.

"Trust me," he assured her. "I don't want to be tied to you any more than you want to be tied to me."

"Always the charmer," she murmured as she glanced out the windshield.

Carson studied her profile. Her beauty couldn't be denied, and neither could the punch of lust to his gut. Attraction wasn't the issue. Carson found many women attractive, but none got under his skin like Lana Langley. Perhaps it was because she not only had the looks, but she also had that independence and drive. She'd gone toe-to-toe with him for the club presidency and he could admit now that they were on the other side, that he'd been worried that she might win. She had the backing of all of the women, considering her position as the chair of the Cattleman's Club Women's Association.

"Did you do this on purpose?" she asked.

Carson jerked back. "What?"

"Did you know what he would think when you decided to come with me?"

Her accusation took a moment to register and Carson couldn't help but laugh. "You think I volunteered to come with you, a visit that was your idea, by the way, all to trap you into an engagement? Honey, don't embarrass yourself."

"Then what do you expect to come from all of this nonsense?" Lana turned toward him once again. "Do you expect me to marry you? Do you expect us to just pretend? How long will that have to go on?"

Lana let out a rich burst of laughter that did nothing to squelch the desire churning in his gut. Even angry and frustrated, she was still damn enticing—not enough that he wanted to be engaged, but here they were.

"Who on earth would believe us in love enough to become engaged?" she added, still laughing. "We were at each other's throats during the campaign, and that's without the infamous family feud."

Carson shook his head. "I have no idea how to pull this off, but did you see his face? I haven't seen him that excited, that surprised and happy, in years. And to know that I was the one who created that joy for him…"

Damn it. He refused to lose it in front of Lana… in front of anyone, really. He couldn't mentally afford to come undone. With his powerful family name and his newly appointed position with the TCC, Carson had to be in control of his emotions at all times.

The last person who could see him as weak was the one person he couldn't get away from.

Lana waited as Carson trailed off and glanced out the side window for a moment. No doubt trying to compose himself.

When he turned back, Carson held her gaze with a fierceness she hadn't seen from him.

"I will do anything for that man," he went on. "Anything. If that means faking this engagement for the next month, then so be it. We pretend to be in love, we go to a party, the money gets donated to the club, and everyone is happy."

Lana laughed. "We'll both be miserable and I don't think you could handle me for that long."

"You think I can't handle you?"

When he reached his arm out to stretch across the back of her seat as he leaned in, Lana's breath caught in her throat. That unwavering dark gaze of his seemed to penetrate through the wall of defense she'd kept up. She had to have that wall, that barrier, between this strong, sexy man and her firm vow to herself that she'd never let another man control her. Not physically or emotionally.

Agreeing to this engagement would be just that. The circumstances would be out of her control… but only temporarily.

"I see your mind working," Carson murmured. "One month, Lana. That's all we need to make this ruse work for everyone."

Why did that husky, gravelly tone make her nerve endings stand at attention? And why did she suddenly have the urge to see if those lips were as soft as they looked?

Finding Carson Wentworth sexy was one thing,

and something she could live with and ignore, but fantasizing about that mouth was a whole other territory she shouldn't venture into.

"And I will have no problem…handling you."

Had he eased closer? Was this space getting smaller? Good heavens, that woodsy cologne seemed to match perfectly with his cropped beard and those heavy lids. The man clearly was made for seduction, and perhaps using his charm was his key mechanism for gaining what he wanted.

But she had her own arsenal of tricks. She wasn't immune to how he looked at her, she wasn't immune to the crackling tension that had started during the campaign and seemed to be growing each day since.

Lana knew, though, that she did have the upper hand here. As much as she wanted those amenities for the women's group, she couldn't accomplish her goal without the new president on board, if she waited him out. But this would be the easiest way, and Carson was right in his assumption that everyone would benefit with a Langley-Wentworth union.

"One month," she agreed, then couldn't help herself and tapped his chin with her index finger. "Not a day more."

He snatched her hand and wrenched it aside as he leaned in closer. That heavy-lidded gaze dropped to her mouth a moment before he offered a naughty grin.

"Perhaps it will be you who's afraid to handle me," he whispered.

Then he turned her hand over until their palms were touching. She could pull back, she could ignore this insistent, invisible tug toward her enemy... but why, when it felt too damn good? When was the last time someone made her nerves tingle with excitement? When was the last time she enjoyed flirty banter?

It had been much too long. In fact, the last time was when she'd entered into what had ultimately become a serious relationship. Well, the joining had been serious on her end until she realized she wasn't being treated the way she deserved.

But that time in her life was over and she refused to allow the negativity to take up any headspace.

"Propose to me."

Carson blinked. "What?"

Lana smiled. "You want me to be your betrothed? Propose."

Carson laughed. "Betrothed? Let's not romanticize this."

"We're in the middle of a family feud and we've made ourselves the sacrifice. Give me some romance, Twenty-Two."

"Is that the type of woman you are?" he asked, taking her hand and examining her fingers one by one. "You said you were the type of woman who wanted to be in charge in a relationship?"

Lana eased back slightly. This was too much. The way he'd manipulated her, this situation…not to mention the manner in which her body kept responding to Carson.

"Oh, I remain in charge, but that doesn't mean I don't want my man to put forth some effort."

"Are you going to be high-maintenance during this engagement?" he asked.

Lana laughed. "I plan on being myself. You still think you can handle me?"

In a swift move she never saw coming, Carson tugged her just close enough that the minuscule space between them was a mere whisper.

"Car—"

His lips closed over hers, not in a forceful, commanding way, but something… Hell, she had no clue how to explain such an unexpected response. New? Curious?

He explored her mouth as if getting to know her, as if taking his time would give him insight to something.

Lana had never been kissed this way before and she'd been convinced that Carson would be a domineering kisser… Yes, she'd thought about it, but she'd never, ever thought he would be so…thorough.

He released her hand as he framed her face, tipping her head just so, right where he wanted it, as he released her for a fraction of a second and then dove back in at a new angle.

She should stop this. Kissing Carson Wentworth was absolute madness. No good could come from acting on the chemistry and attraction. A faux engagement was enough to have her head spinning.

Carson eased back, his hands still secure on her face as his piercing green gaze met hers.

"What was that for?"

Did her voice sound as shaky as she felt? Because somehow the oxygen in the vehicle had all been sucked out and she was having a difficult time breathing.

"This needs to be believable, Lana. If my great-grandfather wants this century-old ax buried, you and I are going to be the ones to bury it."

"We don't even know what battle we're fighting and I never thought I'd team up with you for anything."

Carson dropped his hands, leaving her cool to the touch, which was positively absurd. She didn't crave his touch, nor did she want. She didn't. She just needed to find a date and kiss another man to prove Carson didn't affect her.

But apparently she would have to wait several weeks before that much-needed said date with another man.

"I think this is something we can both agree on," Carson stated. "If that kiss is any indictor, I'd say we can get along for a few weeks in order for the club to receive a very generous sum and to make an old man's dying wish."

Yeah, that last part was actually more important than the money. Lana might have been brought up to hate the Wentworths, but in all honesty, they had done nothing personally to her. Well, Carson was a jerk at times, but that was just his personality.

Harmon was one hundred years old and could die at any time. If his wish was to see this feud cease, then why wouldn't she want to help with that? Other than the fact that everything was a lie.

"This feels wrong," she murmured. "I've never lied in my life."

Carson's eyebrows rose as he eased back a little more. "Never? Not even as a teen?"

Lana curled back. "Never. First of all, I'm a terrible liar. I never saw a reason to back myself into a corner like that and I really don't want to ruin my excellent track record."

Carson nodded. "I get that, and I hate lying to my great-grandfather. But this is something he wants before he dies and we are the only ones who can fulfill that wish. I need your help."

Well, that final statement was sure as hell telling. She'd never known Carson to beg or plead before in her life. Typically, he flashed a smile or tossed money to get what he desired.

"How much did that cost for you to say that?" she joked.

"You have no idea the pain I'm going through knowing I need you in my corner."

Oh, she had a pretty good idea. Realizing she held the upper hand here really did amazing things for her self-esteem…which she appreciated since that dramatic loss by a landslide for the presidency.

"I'll agree to pose as your fiancée if you will immediately start on the women's wing at the clubhouse."

Carson nodded. "Done."

All of this seemed too easy. What was the real hang-up? Posing as a faux engaged couple wouldn't be too difficult. The hardest part would be convincing other people she and Carson were actually in love. But, for that expansion, Lana would do nearly anything. Women deserved just as much private space as the men and there were more female members now than ever before, thanks to her sister-in-law, Abby Langley, who'd opened that door years ago.

Lana fully intended on carrying out what Abby had started and if that meant playing nice with Carson, then so be it. Maybe he'd offer up more of those toe-curling kisses. At least that was something to look forward to, right?

"I'm still waiting on that proposal." Lana reached for her seat belt, silently hinting for him to get going. "People will want to know and I can't make up something like that."

Carson shifted in his seat and started the engine. "I knew this would be a high-maintenance relationship," he murmured.

"Anything worth having is going to take work." Lana reached over and patted his cheek. "If you want me to be your wife, I'm going to need you to give all you've got, Twenty-Two."

He grumbled something else beneath his breath as he pulled out of the parking lot and Lana just smiled as she stared out her window. She had no clue what this next month would bring, but she did know these next few weeks wouldn't be boring.

Four

What the hell had he been thinking kissing her like that? Now that's all he could think of because the damn image wouldn't get out of his head. Lana had always been too sexy for her own good, but he sure as hell hadn't expected her to taste or feel like all of his fantasies rolled into one.

Carson blew out a sigh and headed to the Colt Room for a drink. He'd sent several emails and made some calls regarding contractors for the new women's area. He planned on making good on his promise to Lana, because in turn that would make Harmon happy, and at the end of the day, that's all that mattered.

After that last phone call and then the visitor he'd

had, Carson needed a stiff drink. He'd started off his day with an unwanted interview with Sierra, then had a bomb dropped in his life with that fake engagement to Lana, and now…hell. That ring box was way too damn heavy in his pocket.

As he entered the Colt Room, the instant smell of cigars and bourbon hit him and he felt like he was home. The atmosphere in here just appealed to him more than going home to have a drink.

With the rich wood and the dark steel, the Colt Room definitely lent itself to more of a masculine crowd. Carson could see why Lana wanted to push for the women to have something to call their own.

Perhaps that would be the best way to announce their engagement? Make a huge deal about the addition, as well as their joining the families together.

Carson couldn't think about all of this right now. He just wanted to take a minute to decompress before he moved on to the next stressful portion of his evening.

"Hey, Carson."

Blinking, Carson spotted his cousin Rafael and Rafe's dad, Tobias, at the end of the bar. Had Carson been focused when he walked in, he would have seen them. Granted, the Wentworths were a huge family and there were tons of members in their clan. Carson was glad Rafe and Tobias were finally coming together and getting along after years of being estranged.

He headed toward the end of the glossy mahogany bar and took a seat next to Rafael. Some considered him the black sheep of the family because Rafael had disappeared and done his own thing for years. Going against the family—against Tobias—had never been accepted. The Wentworths were a dynasty of moguls and barons, and breaking from tradition had stunned everyone. Being a world-renowned playboy hadn't helped, either, but now he was back and at the top of the list for the possible father of the abandoned baby found months ago.

Rumors about baby Micah were floating around town as to who could be the biological father, and Sierra was actively trying to identify Micah's dad. The only thing that was certain was that the mystery man was a Cattleman's Club member. That didn't necessarily narrow down the list, considering how many men in Royal, Texas, belonged to the elite establishment.

"How's the new president?" Tobias asked with a wide grin, the gesture creasing the corner of his eyes.

Aside from the fact that he had an unplanned engagement and a lie weighing heavy on his shoulders, things couldn't be better.

"I can't complain," Carson replied. "What are we drinking?"

"Bourbon." Rafael swirled the contents around in his glass. "Let me buy you a drink."

"I wouldn't turn that down."

The bartender came over and Carson chose a top-shelf bourbon before turning back to the guys.

"So what brought both of you out to the club on a Monday evening?"

Tobias adjusted his Stetson and shrugged. "We decided to meet here for a drink to unwind from the day. We'll probably end up eating dinner here."

The usually confident Tobias looked at Rafe. Obviously, they were still unsure of where they stood with each other and whether dinner together might be pushing it.

When Rafael nodded, Tobias turned back to Carson and said, "You're more than welcome to join us."

Carson would much rather have dinner with them as opposed to what he actually needed to do. That damn box in his pocket mocked him and he really had nobody to blame but himself. Had he just let Lana go visit Harmon on her own, there would have been no misunderstanding.

But there wasn't much he could do now to untangle the web of lies he'd started.

"Thanks, but I can only stay for a drink."

The bartender set his tumbler on the bar and moved back down to the group of men who'd just entered. Before Carson could take his first sip, Rafael jerked up from his stool and grabbed his cell off the bar.

"Excuse me. I've been waiting on this call."

Whatever it was, it must be something big, Carson mused. Rafe stepped off into the corner and raked a hand through his hair. Carson tried not to pay too much attention as he took a sip of his bourbon, but Tobias couldn't peel his eyes away.

After a moment, Rafael came back and slapped his hand on the bar top with a soft chuckle. "The next round is on me, guys."

"Good news?" Carson asked.

"You could say that. The DNA tests results are finally in and, as I've been saying, I'm not the father of Micah."

"I never thought you were the father," Tobias stated. "But I'm glad you have the proof. So who does that leave for them to look at next?"

Rafael shrugged as he took a seat back on the leather stool. "I have no clue, and now that Micah's mom, Arielle, is gone, there's no one to tell the truth. But whoever he is, I'm afraid he'll get raked over the coals from the people in this town for abandoning a pregnant woman and then not coming forward."

"Maybe he never knew she was pregnant," Carson added.

"That has to be the reason," Tobias agreed. "Regardless of who it is, someone's life is about to change dramatically."

Carson had his own issues to deal with and an infant was not one of them. The baby was in good hands, and right now, that's the best anyone could hope for.

"So what are your plans?" he asked Rafael. "Are you planning on leaving town or sticking around for a while?"

Rafael gripped his glass and shifted in his seat to face Carson. "Actually, I'm looking to open a luxe guest ranch as an investment property. I think something like that would really bring more people to Royal and produce a nice profit."

Carson nodded. "That sounds like a great plan. Certainly something the town could use."

"Nothing is official yet, I'm still just in the planning stages," Rafael added. "Hopefully this won't be long to turn into a reality."

Carson picked up his tumbler and tossed back the rest of his bourbon, welcoming the familiar burn. He needed a little courage right now. Which was ridiculous. He wasn't afraid of Lana…but he was afraid of the emotions she pulled from him.

The unwanted, disturbing, terrifying emotions. He wanted her. Plain and simple—or maybe not so plain and simple. Perhaps this was all complex and disorderly for all he knew. They'd just started on this path together and they still had the entire month left to go.

"I appreciate the drink." Carson got to his feet and tossed a couple bucks on the bar for the bartender. "I have to meet someone in a bit. It was good to see you both."

Tobias tipped his hat and Rafael nodded with a smile. Carson made his way out of the Colt Room and out of the clubhouse. The lot was full, which was the norm. At nearly any time of the day or evening, the Cattleman's Club was hopping. With all the amenities, the restaurant and the bar, there was something for everyone.

And there would be even more for the ladies once he and Lana went forward with their engagement…or at least pretended to. She'd make that ladies' lounge top priority the moment that money changed hands and was passed over to the club.

Why was he so nervous to head to Lana's house? He didn't plan on doing anything other than handing her the ring and leaving. That's all. Just to make everything look official before they went public with this farce.

The sun had already set and Carson turned off the main street through Royal, heading toward Lana's home on the edge of town.

Obviously, over the next several weeks they would both be venturing into new territory and spending more time together.

Their ruse had to look legit. Lying to his great-grandfather already had a heavy stone of guilt resting in his gut—the last thing he needed was to be caught in the lie.

For the second time today, Carson pulled into Lana's circle drive and killed the engine. He stared at the stone-and-wood home with the tall peak over the wide porch. A light inside the front door shone bright and another light at the end of the house was also on. She was awake. Maybe he should have called or texted. Hell, something to warn her he was coming.

He muttered a curse beneath his breath as he stepped from his SUV. He was dropping off a damn ring. That was all.

But mercy, what would she be wearing? Because she continually killed him with those damn body-hugging outfits. Those curves she had made him want to forget there'd ever been any feud, or that they now had a fake engagement. One night. That's all he wanted and then maybe he'd get Lana Langley out of his system.

Carson reached the porch and her front door swung open. Lana was standing there wearing a short robe and a crooked smile with one eyebrow raised.

Hell. He definitely should've called. This was a bad, bad idea.

Carson headed onto the porch, anyway, adrenaline and arousal pumping through him...totally ignoring the warning bells.

Five

Lana's driveway alarm had chimed through her house and echoed onto her patio just as she'd stepped from the hot tub and tied her robe. She'd dried off her feet and padded through the open area toward her front door. A quick peek through the etched glass and she knew who that strong build belonged to. She shouldn't have been surprised to see Carson on her doorstep, but she was.

Lana flicked her locks, opened the door wide, and gripped the edge of the wood as she stared at her unexpected guest.

The shadowy darkness combined with the slash of brightness from her porch light made him appear even more intriguing, sexy, and much too attractive for her to be noticing…especially half-dressed.

"Did I catch you at a bad time?" he asked.

"I just stepped out of the hot tub."

His shoulder relaxed as he took another step toward her. "For a second I thought I got you out of the shower and you had nothing on beneath that robe."

Lana laughed and propped one hand on her hip and one hand on the door. "I don't have anything on under the robe," she replied. "I live alone out in the country and have a private patio."

Carson's eyes widened a fraction, then they raked down her body. Maybe she should have kept that kernel of information to herself. The words had just escaped, and now with the way Carson's hungry gaze was traveling all over her body, she wondered what she had done. Like she needed more of a reason to be attracted to her temporary, fake fiancé.

"What are you doing here?" she asked, hoping to circle back to his reason for dropping by.

He continued to stare at her and Lana dropped her arms to her sides. Carson took another step closer, now coming fully into the light. Maybe he should've stayed in the partial shadow because now she could see every chiseled feature, the square jaw covered in stubble, the heavy-lidded stare, those piercing green eyes.

There was an intensity to him she'd never seen

before. This wasn't oil-tycoon Carson or new-club-president Carson...this was Carson, the man who clearly couldn't hide his desire.

"Do you always answer your door nearly naked?" he asked, his voice husky.

That low tone sent shivers through her and made her think of a darkened room and rumpled sheets. But she shouldn't be thinking of any such fantasy... at least not with Carson Wentworth.

"I'm not at all naked," she countered. "And believe it or not, I'm not naive. I looked out before opening the door. I didn't think you were here to rob me."

Carson closed the final few inches between them, causing Lana to tip back her head to hold his stare. She wasn't sure if he was trying to intimidate her, turn her on, or throw his masculine weight around. No matter what, Lana had to remain on her toes and in control...because she was about one more sexy statement away from ripping the tie from her robe and begging.

"What did you think I was here for?" he asked.

Lana licked her lips, another mistake. His eyes darted to her mouth and she honestly had not meant to do anything to draw his attention to any other parts of her body. It's just that her mouth had gone dry.

"I don't want to play games, Carson."

His lips quirked. "You said my name."

Confused, she jerked slightly, then remembered she'd been calling him by that silly nickname. Perhaps she should have stuck with that, but his name just slid through her lips.

"Why do you have to drive me crazy?"

She shifted her attention to the muttered statement he'd just made.

"What?" she asked.

Carson shook his head and raked a hand over the back of his neck. "You drive me crazy, okay? You have to know that."

"That's nothing new," she retorted. "We've driven each other crazy for—"

The man moved fast…too fast. One second he was staring at her and the next one he had his hands on her face and was backing her into her house, with his mouth on hers. Lana gripped his shoulders—to prevent herself from stumbling or to get closer, she wasn't sure.

Damn, but he could kiss. He towered over her, he consumed her, he made her feel so feminine. She shouldn't find his commanding approach so attractive, but she couldn't help herself.

Carson pulled away just as abruptly as he'd come on to her. He cursed beneath his breath and turned away, staring back out the open front door. Was he ready to run? Was he having regrets?

Lana waited for him to finish whatever internal battle he seemed to be having with himself.

She needed a minute herself to figure out why she craved Carson's kisses like those of no other man she'd ever been with.

"I didn't come here for this."

He took a step, closed the door, and then turned back to face her. That hunger in his eyes hadn't disappeared—if anything, the fire seemed to have flared even higher.

"I tried to talk myself out of any contact with you tonight and just having you come to my office tomorrow. Then I had a drink in the Colt Room and ultimately decided to do this now, when I knew we'd be alone."

He cocked his head to the side in that adorable way that she found much too sexy.

"Being alone isn't the best idea, though," he added.

"Why is that?"

"Is that a rhetorical question?"

No, but she wanted him to say it. She wanted to force him to say what he was thinking, what he was feeling.

"There's too much between us," he murmured. "The history, the engagement, the tension."

She took a step toward him. "Yet you showed up at my house at night without a warning. Makes me wonder if you were curious what would happen."

A muscle in his jaw clenched as his lips thinned and his nostrils flared. Oh, the man was tempted and furious about it. Well, that made two of them. She couldn't deny her attraction—what would be the point? Ignoring something wouldn't make it go away… If anything, she would just be even more agitated and aroused than usual.

Even during the debates and electoral process, she found Carson infuriating, yet sexy and powerful. Of course, she never admitted that to anyone, really not even to herself, but again, she couldn't ignore the glaring facts.

In a move she didn't expect or see coming, Carson reached out and snaked an arm around her waist. Lana tumbled right against his chest and flattened her palms against him to hold on.

"What if I did wonder?" he muttered as his gaze dropped to her mouth. "What if I need to get you out of my system?"

Lana slid her hands along his shoulders and around his neck, threading her fingers through his hair. She tipped up her head as her entire body ached for him to rip away these barriers between them—the clothes and the rivalry. Just for one night. Would that be too much to ask?

"Be sure," she told him. "Because I'm about a second away from tearing this robe off and showing you exactly what you want."

Carson's lids lowered as he rested his forehead against hers. "Your confidence is the sexiest thing about you, right next to this damn body I need to get my hands on."

Well, say no more. Finally, something truly raw and honest from his mouth.

Lana took a step back and slid the knot loose on her robe, all the while keeping her eyes locked on his. She wanted to see his face—she needed to see his face as she undressed before him.

And he was right. She was confident and loved her body, and she couldn't wait for him to show her just how much he'd been wanting her. They'd been doing the visual foreplay dance for months now and there was no reason they couldn't just take what they wanted. Why should either of them let a century-old feud rob them of a night of passion?

As the robe slid silently to puddle at her feet, Carson's eyes seemed to rake all over her and Lana's entire body heated with arousal.

"Just for tonight." He took a step closer, then another, until there was nothing between them. "You're mine for tonight."

Without a word, she started working on the buttons of his shirt, until one proved to be difficult, so she yanked the material, sending the troublesome button flinging to the other side of the room.

"You're killing me," he growled.

Carson took over, and within seconds, he stood before her wearing nothing but a hungry gaze. He gripped her waist, lifted her, and carried her toward the living area. Lana wrapped her legs and arms around him, turned on even more by his strength and dominance.

She'd envisioned this moment way too many times. A fantasy with Carson as the star had consumed her thoughts much more than she should have ever allowed.

But she wasn't sorry this was happening and she didn't give a damn about the red flags waving around in her mind.

Would this complicate their fake engagement? Doubtful. It's not like they'd vowed any solid, long-term promises to each other.

"I haven't exactly been immune to you, either," she retorted. "But I'm done talking."

She cupped the back of his neck and pulled his mouth down to hers, then found herself tipping backward until her back hit the cushy sofa. Carson's weight came on top of hers, pressing her deeper into the couch, and she'd never imagined how glorious this would feel. Well, she'd imagined, but nothing could have prepared her for exactly how amazing this was.

And she couldn't help but have a bit of a thrill knowing this entire charade was a secret between them. Nobody had to know their relationship was fake, but their one-night stand was oh, so very real.

Carson's mouth slid from her lips, along her jawline, and down the column of her neck. Lana arched back to allow him better access. No way was she denying those talented lips. She'd waited too long to have them roaming over her body.

When the stubble of his beard raked over her nipple, Lana shivered and clutched his shoulders. Gracious sakes, this man was hitting all of her delicious spots and they'd barely gotten started.

"Wait," she panted.

Carson lifted his head. Those full, damp lips were too damn tempting, but she wasn't one to rush into anything...save for this moment. But, she still had to be smart.

"I don't have any protection," she told him. "I'm on birth control and I've never gone without, but..."

There were a whole host of other things they could do, but she'd been wanting the real deal.

"I have something."

Carson eased from her body and crossed the room to where he'd left his pants by the door. He pulled out his wallet and grabbed the protection.

Lana couldn't tear her eyes away from that fine form of muscle tone and lean man. Carson made his suits look good. He made a pair of jeans and cowboy boots look sexy. But seeing him in her own living room wearing nothing but a bedroom stare was flat-out toe-curling and panty-melting...well, if she had any panties on.

As he crossed back to her, completely ready now, Lana got to her feet and gestured toward the sofa.

"Sit," she commanded.

Carson's dark eyebrows rose as he quirked those lips into a grin. "That bossy attitude is much sexier here than during the debates."

He stood in front of her and she placed her hands on his chest and eased him down until he sat. Those hungry eyes kept her attention as she settled her knees on either side of his waist, braced her hands on his shoulders, and hovered just over where she ached most to be.

"Not bossy," she corrected. "Determined."

Without another word, she joined their bodies and stilled. Carson's hands gripped her waist as he let out a low groan. Lana just needed a moment to adjust to this amazing sensation. She'd wanted to take control, but that grasp was slowly slipping away.

When his hips jerked beneath hers, Lana shifted, working into a rhythm that couldn't be contained or controlled. She'd wanted to go slow, to savor this come-to-life fantasy. But she needed him too bad and she wasn't going to deny herself any longer.

Carson's hands traveled from her waist up to her chest. The second he palmed her in each hand, Lana arched her back, seeking his touch. When his mouth replaced his hands, Lana cried out and shifted her gaze to watch him. She framed the side of his face, holding him exactly where she needed. To feel Carson all around her, to be consumed by this man, was more than she could bear.

Every euphoric sensation bubbled up and overcame her. She curled her fingers into that taut skin over his shoulders and quickened her pace. She needed more, craved more.

Carson released her breasts and framed her face, pulling her in for a kiss. He covered her mouth with his as she went over the edge. That was it. That was what she needed. Just that basic connection of a passionate kiss from the man she'd been dreaming about.

Carson's body tightened beneath hers and Lana poured herself into the kiss, drawing out his own pleasure. She wanted him to feel just as much as she did…and part of her admitted she didn't want this night to end. He broke from the kiss and tipped his back head, giving her the most spectacular view of his undoing. The man was positively gorgeous when he became vulnerable.

When Carson stilled beneath her, Lana eased off his lap, but he grabbed hold of her hips. In a swift, clever move, she found herself on her back with him hovering over her. That naughty grin only had another stirring of arousal curling through her.

"Where are you going?" he asked.

"I thought—"

"We said one night." He grazed his lips across hers. "And the night just got started."

Six

Lana rolled over in her bed, not surprised to find it empty. Still, that didn't stop the disappointment from hitting her. They had agreed on one night, but part of her just assumed he'd at least hang around for coffee, or at the very least a simple goodbye.

But she wasn't going to dwell on what didn't happen because she was still feeling all sorts of amazing from what *did* happen.

Lana reached for her phone, but remembered she had other things on her mind and she hadn't brought it to bed. Carson had carried her in here with ease and his strength was just another major turn-on. How could she not thrive in the fact a man could handle her physically and mentally?

Stretching her arms over her head, Lana swung her legs over the side of the bed and pushed aside last night. She'd given herself that one pleasurable time and now she needed to move on and shift her focus to the women's area that Carson promised to build with the funds from Harmon.

Which reminded her, they also needed to plan the engagement party. Well, she would plan it because she had control issues and she wanted everything to be perfect. Not to mention the fact that the party was the place they were going to announce the new expansion for the women's facilities. She couldn't wait to tell Abby about this.

Even though Lana's brother, Richard, had passed away, Lana had gained a true sister when Abby had married him. Lana shared everything with her sister-in-law, even though she was now remarried and so happy and in love. Lana was thrilled that she'd found her second chance.

Abby had been the pioneer of getting women into the club in the first place, so Lana was beyond anxious to fill in Abby on the plans. Should those plans also mention the fake engagement?

As much as she wanted to spill all to Abby, Lana figured it was best that this secret stayed between her and Carson. If word leaked at all and somehow got back to Harmon, the funds would be gone and the dying wish of a man would be destroyed.

Lana reached for her robe on the antique trunk at

the end of her bed. Good thing she had a few robes because her other one was still in a silky puddle at her front door.

As she padded through the living room, heading for the kitchen and much-needed coffee, she couldn't ignore the flood of memories from last night...or the sight. There was the robe just like she recalled. The couch cushions were a little askew and she couldn't help but stare, her body heating up all over again.

The things they'd done on that couch had been nothing compared to what had happened when Carson took over in the bedroom. How could she not want a replay of all of that?

She could want, but she couldn't have. They'd made an agreement, right?

When she turned back toward the kitchen she spied her cell on the island and a small blue box next to it. Confused, Lana crossed the space and picked up the box. The second she lifted the lid, she gasped.

The most incredible diamond-and-pearl ring stared back at her and she had no clue what it was doing here...but she had an idea who had left it.

Lana picked up her cell and noticed a missed text from Carson. When she opened it, her heart clenched a bit...and not in the sweet, romantic way.

Your engagement ring I meant to give you last night, but got sidetracked. We need to focus and keep the goal in mind.

She glanced back to the ring once again and suddenly the beauty of it seemed almost tarnished. Even though they had agreed on the one heated night, that didn't mean she wanted a cold, lonely morning.

She closed the lid on the box and didn't bother replying to the message. As much as she wanted to slide that beauty on her hand, she wasn't quite feeling this proposal. Granted it was fake, but he could have at least...

Hell, she didn't know. What did she want him to do? Get down on one knee with a candlelight dinner and then whisk her off to bed? What was the protocol for a proposal for a fake engagement?

She knew this wasn't reality, but couldn't he have put forth a little effort to pretend she wasn't just some one-night stand? All of this was such new territory for both of them, but she still had feelings and as much as she hated to admit it, she did want romance...even if that had to be a show as well.

Lana tried to ignore that pang of frustration as she got ready for the day. She opted to spend a little extra time on her makeup and hair, and she chose a killer black suit with a jacket that nipped at her waist and had matching pencil pants. Solid red pumps completed her look and she felt much more like herself than she had just an hour ago.

Getting ready was more for herself and the temporary fiancé she'd be seeing today. She never dressed for anyone else other than herself and sometimes her wounded pride needed to step it up a notch.

Lana grabbed her favorite handbag and gave that box another glare. She slid her cell into her bag and tossed the ring box in, too. Maybe a meeting with her "betrothed" would be best before she let her emotions swelter and she exploded. Because the more she thought about it, the angrier she became that he'd just left this ring like some parting gift after their night together.

Once she was in her car, she started rehearsing just what she'd say to her beloved fiancé.

"Sure, Dad. Sounds good."

Carson leaned back in his leather office chair and turned to stare out the wide window that offered him a view of the grounds behind the clubhouse, where the stables were located. He'd barely gotten in the office before his father, Hank, had called to invite him for dinner tomorrow night.

"Will you be bringing a date?" his dad asked.

Carson nearly cringed. Should he bring Lana? They were going to have to announce this engagement soon, but he was going to have to text Lana before he committed to anything with his family.

"Not sure about that," Carson replied. "You know I'm not one to bring my dates around the family."

"I heard you were engaged."

That unexpected punch to his gut came out of nowhere, but Carson couldn't let his dad know he'd caught him off guard.

"I see you've talked to Harmon."

"I stopped by last night and he informed me you have a very interesting story, which is why I called you about dinner."

Of course. So asking about the date had been a leading question. He was going to have to tell Lana it was game on from this point forward and they needed to get their stories matching, because there would sure as hell be questions as to how a Wentworth and a Langley had managed to "fall in love."

"I'll save the story for dinner entertainment," Carson promised.

No way would he say anything without talking to Lana first.

"I better see Ms. Langley at my doorstep with you tomorrow," his father warned. "I had no idea you two were even talking friendly toward each other, let alone ready to spend your life with her."

Movement from the corner of his eye caught his attention. Carson spun his chair and spotted his fiancée…who didn't seem as happy to see him as she had last night, when she'd stripped out of her robe. Hadn't she seen the gorgeous ring he'd left for her? How could anyone be upset with that?

"I'll see you tomorrow, Dad." Carson got to his feet. "Someone just came into my office."

"Bring Ms. Langley."

Carson didn't reply as he ended the call and slid the cell onto his desktop. His eyes met Lana's and he offered a smile.

"Morning." His focus shifted to her hand…and bare finger. "Didn't you see the ring?"

Lana laughed, but there was no humor and suddenly he had a gut feeling she wasn't too happy with him.

"Oh, I saw it." She sat her handbag in the leather chair across from his desk and pulled out the ring box. "Here it is. And, while it's lovely, your proposal sucks."

Confused, Carson leaned back in his chair and continued to stare across to Lana's fiery gaze. He much preferred her heated look from last night as opposed to this one. Clearly something about the ring had set her off. And the proposal… What the hell?

"You are aware this is a fake engagement, right?"

"You are aware I told you I needed a real proposal because I'm a terrible liar." She opened the lid on the ring box, yanked out the ring and circled his desk. "People will want to know our story and we have to get this together."

Agreed, but damn it. What had she done to her hair and makeup? There was something sultry… something sexier, like she'd just gotten out of her lover's bed.

Oh, wait…

And that curve-hugging suit made him want to lock his office door and familiarize himself all over again with all of that smooth, silky skin beneath his touch.

Lana dropped to one knee. "Will you marry me?"

Carson stared down at her and way too many fantasies came to mind with her looking like a vixen in that position. But they'd agreed on one night and they'd gotten that out of their systems. Right?

He had to keep his eye on the goal of the funds from Harmon that would benefit the entire club.

"Are you asking me?"

Lana nodded. "Someone needs to do the asking. Now, put the ring on my finger."

Carson reached for the ring, keeping his eyes locked on hers the entire time. He slid the ring on, then got to his feet, tugging her up with him. Clutching her hand between the two of them, he cupped the side of her face with his free hand.

"Lana, let's put this century-old feud to rest. Will you help me build a dynasty that only we could and help our families move on once and for all?"

Her eyes widened and he wondered if he'd gone too far. He wondered, after last night, if Lana's feelings for him had changed. He couldn't afford for hearts to get involved here—*they* couldn't afford it. Two headstrong people actually trying to have a relationship? They'd never make it—not when both needed full control.

"If you don't say yes, I will."

Carson jerked his attention to the doorway, where Sierra was standing with a bright smile on her face, her eyes darting between Carson and Lana.

Lana eased her hand from between them and met his gaze for a brief second before she pasted a smile on her face and turned toward their unexpected guest.

"You caught us," Lana stated with a soft laugh. "We were trying to keep it a secret for a little while, but I guess that would be difficult to do."

Sierra stepped into the office, her eyes wide as she shook her head. "I just can't believe this. I mean, you two were so opposite during the debates. But I saw that spark every time you were together. Did you guys have a secret fling going on during that time?"

Oh, no. All of that frustration and their rivalry had been one-hundred-percent real…just like the battle between their families.

"That's when we realized we were perfect for each other," Carson replied. "We figured this wedge between our families could end with us, and despite both wanting the presidency of the club, we have quite a bit in common."

Lana glanced to him, eyebrows quirked, as if silently asking him what exactly they had in common.

Well, there was their shared fiery passion, but probably best not to mention that to Sierra. Who knew what would end up printed or online?

"This is absolutely wonderful news," Sierra gushed. "Can I get an exclusive or do you have something planned for a big announcement?"

Carson glanced to Lana. Even though this entire charade was a farce, he didn't want to disrespect Lana or do anything that would harm the deal they'd made. She gave him a slight nod before turning her attention back to Sierra.

"We wouldn't mind an exclusive with you," Lana told her. "We haven't really told our families yet, but we can schedule something."

"Tomorrow morning?" Sierra asked, hope lacing her tone as her eyes darted between them. "I can meet you here around ten and we could do a short interview, but I'd love to get some pictures."

"I'm fine with that," Lana told her.

Carson nodded. "Sounds good. What did you need today?"

Sierra blinked. "What? Oh, right. I forgot when I saw that touching engagement. You two must really be in love."

So far, so good. Getting their families to believe this crazy scheme was one thing, but having a busybody reporter running a story was actually going to be a big deal. With Sierra already convinced, there was no doubt she'd come up with a gushing write-up for them tomorrow, and once the people of Royal caught wind of the engagement, there would be absolutely no turning back.

Not that he was going to, anyway, but this was getting even more serious and those nerves in his gut were becoming damn uncomfortable. Lying to his great-grandfather, lying to his father, now lying to the town he loved and the people who trusted him. He'd built a solid reputation, which was how he'd secured the club presidency, and now he was lying to everyone…except the woman who should be his enemy, yet had turned into his lover.

How the hell had this gotten so skewed?

"I came by to see if you cared if I went to visit Harmon," Sierra continued. "I promise to be gentle with my questions, but after reading Arielle's diary and talking to most of the people of Royal, I wouldn't be a very good investigative reporter if I didn't interview him personally. I'm hoping Arielle told him something about Micah's father."

"Why didn't you just call?" he asked.

"I'm actually meeting someone for a horse-riding lesson in the stables shortly, so I thought I'd just swing by and ask in person."

Carson mulled over the idea and he completely understood why she'd want to see Harmon. Even though his great-grandfather was still in his right mind, he was one hundred years old and his time was limited. But he liked Sierra. He had no reason to believe she wasn't trying to find out the entire story, and show Royal and the entire town in the best light.

Carson had always been a good judge of character, so he trusted Sierra, and he didn't trust just anybody. For example, he wasn't sure he trusted the woman wearing his ring whom he'd spent the night with…but that was a whole other issue he didn't want to think about right now.

"I believe you have baby Micah and Harmon's best interests at heart," Carson stated. "The way you keep working every angle makes me see you actually want to uncover the truth. I don't mind if you interview him. I'll call to let them know you're coming."

Sierra beamed. "Thank you, thank you. I'll see you both in the morning, and congrats on the engagement. This is so exciting."

She spun on her booted heel and swept out of the office, leaving Carson and Lana alone once again. Perhaps alone wasn't the best place for them to be, not with the images and the emotions running high from last night.

He'd thought that being intimate with her would have satisfied his wants and he could have moved on, but those wants had only grown into a fierce, aching need. That's why he'd left so early, without a word. He'd left the ring and sent a text because if he'd stayed at her place and waited for her to open those gorgeous eyes, he would have had to have had her all over again. And that wasn't in their business arrangement.

Seven

The ring on her finger seemed so foreign, so wrong. That twinge of pain she'd felt this morning upon seeing it seemed to grow. She'd been so focused on her duties as chair of the Cattleman's Club Women's Association for so many years, she just hadn't had time to date much. But she did want a husband and a family. She'd dreamed of having a sprawling ranch and a sexy, Southern gentleman who could match her wits and strength.

And while Carson certainly fit that criteria, this life wasn't real. The ring meant nothing in the grand scheme of things.

"We're having dinner with my father tomorrow evening at the ranch."

Carson's words pulled her from her thoughts and she turned to focus on the man who'd turned her world, and emotions, upside down.

"Was that a question or a demand?" she asked.

"It was a fact," he informed her. "I'm not thrilled with taking you to dinner, either, but this is the role we both have to play."

Lana rolled her eyes and stepped around his desk, putting distance between them again. "I'm feeling so welcome already."

Carson blew out a sigh as he unbuttoned the sleeves of his black dress shirt and rolled up the cuffs. When he glanced back her way, he caught her staring at his bare forearms.

Why did she have to find everything sexy about him now? He'd been sexy yesterday morning, too, but after last night, well…

She was in serious trouble here.

"This isn't about our feelings or our comfort zone," he reminded her. "We're doing this for Harmon as a dying wish, not to mention the club and all of the funds that will be coming in. This will help my reputation as president and get you what you want with the women's portion of the club, so you'll maintain good standings with our female ranchers. It's all business, Lana."

Business, yes. She knew that. She did…but that didn't stop her from wanting him again. Last night hadn't been enough and she'd been a fool for thinking one night would get someone like Carson Wentworth out of her system. The man exuded everything she found sexy: confidence, power, wit, and he was beyond attractive…and now she could add "amazing lover" to the ever-growing list of gold-star qualities.

They weren't meant to be and she was letting naive thoughts override common sense here. A hot body, a powerful man, and great sex did not make the foundation of a solid relationship. Well, those certainly helped, but trust was certainly a main factor and she couldn't really trust a Wentworth. She'd been brought up hearing "those damn Wentworths" at her kitchen table for the past thirty plus years.

Her parents were simply going to be in utter shock when she broke the news to them, which was something she needed to do before speaking with Sierra in the morning.

"I'm all for getting what we both want," she told Carson. "And I think now that Sierra saw my proposal to you, that will help start that rumor mill."

"I proposed to you," he corrected.

Lana laughed. "I didn't see you getting down on one knee."

"I left the ring and a text."

"And people wonder why you were still single," she muttered. "Anyway, I'm meeting with one more local contractor this afternoon to go over my ideas. I'll get his quote and then discuss everything that was in my original email with you, hopefully by the end of the week."

Carson's dark eyebrows rose. "You move fast."

"Considering yesterday morning you were my enemy, last night you were my lover, and this morning you're my fiancé, I'd say that's the theme as of late."

Carson laughed and raked a hand down the stubble along his jawline. That bristling sound against his palm had shivers racing through her body. She knew exactly how that coarse hair felt against her bare skin and, honestly, she wasn't opposed to asking him for a replay of the night before.

Right now, though, they needed to focus on business and kicking off the announcement of their engagement. Sex could wait—not for long, but it could wait until she was sure her head was on straight and no more emotions other than physical attraction would get in the way.

"We also need to discuss the engagement party at the end of the month," she told him. "Let's have a dance. I've put together a spreadsheet of all the necessary contacts and what I would need from each one."

"When did you have time to do that?" he asked.

"Before you came over and ended up in my bed."

Carson's lids lowered, his lips thinned, and that muscle in his jaw clenched. Perfect. Good to know he wasn't immune to what happened. Likely he was sorting out his own feelings, which was why she was giving him some time before she invited him back for round two.

"I'm too busy to plan a dance, so I'll trust you on that," he told her. "Just tell me the date and I'll make sure the ballroom is cleared for the day."

"I already cleared it," she told him. "And I'll take care of everything. Just wondering if you had any special requests. Your favorite song, a party food you'd love, a color dress I should wear?"

"Green," he said without hesitation. "My favorite color is green. I don't care what else you do."

She should've known the color of money was his favorite color, but if he wanted green, then she'd find a killer dress in a beautiful shade. This might be a fake relationship, but that didn't mean she couldn't look like the stylish queen she prided herself on being.

Lana would have to put in a call to her favorite designer as soon as she left the office. This was going to be her engagement party, after all.

"I'll see you tomorrow morning, then."

Lana grabbed her bag from the chair, turned on her heel, and headed toward the door.

"Wait."

Carson's command stopped her before she could make her exit. She glanced over her shoulder and met his heavy-lidded gaze across the room. With those dark jeans that hugged his narrow hips and that dress shirt with the sleeves rolled up, he looked more like a Royal rancher than the Cattleman's Club president. Both sides of him were starting to appeal to her way too much.

"About last night…"

Lana used every ounce of her willpower to keep her thoughts and words inside while she waited on him to finish his thought.

"I lied," he told her. "Once wasn't enough."

Lana smiled. "No. It wasn't. I'll see you tonight."

Eight

"I can honestly say I never thought this day would come."

Lana cringed at Hank Wentworth's statement the moment he swung open the front door of the family ranch.

"You thought I'd never want to settle down?" Carson asked.

"Never," his father said with a shake of his head. "And to a Langley, of all things. I can't wait to hear how all of this came about. Come on in."

Carson slid his hand over the small of Lana's back and escorted her inside. She had every desire to turn around and wait in the car. Clearly, Hank was going to be a tough nut to crack. But Lana felt solid in their scheme.

After their passionate night back at her house and their interview with Sierra this morning, Lana was ready for the real test—convincing Hank Wentworth that she was madly in love with his son and they were going to forge the families together for life.

A burning of guilt gnawed at her. She hadn't been joking when she said she was a terrible liar. She was so bad at it because she loathed lying and couldn't pull it off.

She didn't want to get into the reasons with Carson, or anyone else for that matter, as to why she couldn't tolerate anything less than honesty.

Yet here she was in this web of deceit because sex and money had lured her in. Part of her knew she was doing this to better the clubhouse and get everything she'd promised her female ranchers, but another part felt she was no different than her father.

When this month was over, Lana vowed to never lie again, and she truly hoped Carson did most of the speaking during this family dinner. She didn't know him well enough to know if he was skilled at stretching the truth, or if such things even bothered him.

"Whatever you have cooking smells amazing," Carson stated as they made their way through the grand foyer and toward the back of the house.

"I had the chef prepare all of your favorites." Hank

glanced over his shoulder and smiled. "Alli and Tate are here, too. Alli is ready to discuss wedding plans, so don't disappoint her. But first, I want to hear all about how this crazy engagement came to be."

Carson tensed beside her and Lana wished they had both come up with some excuse as to why they couldn't attend tonight's dinner...or at least a reason why she couldn't.

She could only assume Hank didn't care what impression he made on her in a more personal setting. She'd only encountered him on occasion at the club, or during the presidential race. But this was the first time she'd ever been in the Wentworth estate and she might as well have been walking into a waiting room full of people waiting on a colonoscopy.

"Oh, my word. You're here."

Alli Wentworth came around the large kitchen island with her arms extended and heading straight for Lana. Suddenly she found herself pulled into an embrace, something she wasn't used to by near strangers and definitely not something she expected from Hank's wife.

"We are so excited for you guys," Alli exclaimed as she eased back. "You are just so stunning. Carson is one lucky man."

"Yes, he is," Lana agreed easily. "It's good to remind him of that."

"Where's Tate?" Carson asked, clearly not wanting to discuss just how lucky he was for having Lana as his fiancée.

"He's out back on the phone with his girlfriend." Alli gestured toward another room. "Let's head into the dining room. He'll come in when they're done arguing. It's that crazy teenage love right now."

Lana remembered her teen boyfriend and the petty arguments they would have. She remembered that sense of freedom when she broke up with him, too.

Carson guided her into the dining room, and that hand on the small of her back did nothing to stop the nerves from swirling around in her belly. Which was so ridiculous, really. The things they'd done in that hot tub of hers last night alone would be enough to make anyone blush. Yet the simple gesture of the way that he was firmly escorting her had those giddy schoolgirl feelings bubbling to the surface.

"Have a seat anywhere you like," Alli told them.

Lana glanced at the spread and couldn't believe all the food. Steaks, mashed potatoes, grilled asparagus wrapped in bacon, a nice big bowl of fresh salad, homemade bread, and a plate of cheeses and fruits.

Lana was glad she'd skipped lunch today, but she'd only done so because she was nervous about coming here. Another thing that was completely ridiculous. She never got nervous about anything, not since she realized her worth and her value at a young age. But this whole charade had her on edge…or maybe it was the good sex that had her out of sorts.

Either way, all of it would come to an end in one short month.

"So let's hear how you both went from being at each other's throats to planning to spend your lives together."

Hank's judgmental tone had Lana straightening her spine. She didn't care to answer his questions, but she was certainly going to let Carson have the first shot at any. Lana had dealt with high-and-mighty men before—some women, too—so this was nothing new. She just had to put on her proverbial suit of armor and prepare herself for a verbal battle.

"We just realized that we did have quite a bit in common, but we simply had different ways of saying it or going about our goals," Carson began. "It's no secret I've always found Lana beautiful, but the more I got to know her mind, the more I fell in love with that strength and determination. I found that she matched me in too many ways to ignore."

Lana tried to block out what he'd said, seeing as it was all part of a hoax, but ignoring his convincing statement was damn difficult. Aside from what Carson had said, the man was also sitting so close that his thigh was resting against hers beneath the table…

He certainly had a way of making her feel like

she was the one. If she didn't know this was fake, she'd start believing Carson really did have a thing for her. He was putting on a great show here already and the two nights they'd spent together had quickly solidified him as the best lover she'd ever had.

"So just a few months of running for club president and you've already put a ring on her finger?" Hank asked.

Alli started around the table filling everyone's plates. Clearly Hank's second wife loved entertaining and she was the quintessential Southern-hospitality hostess.

"As I said, we have quite a bit in common and I can't help who I fall in love with." Carson eased over to let Alli reach through. "Marriages have been based on less than what Lana and I have already. We're both determined and stubborn enough to make this work. Neither one of us want to fail at anything, let alone a marriage."

Damn. He was good. Did lying come that easily to him? One right after another just rolled off his tongue and there was no way in hell Lana could fall for someone who could fabricate such a convincing story with ease. Her father had been the same and her mother had been a fool, or naive, or simply didn't care. Lana vowed to never turn a blind eye, as her mother had.

"Is this some publicity stunt?" Hank asked.

"Oh, really," Alli scolded. "Leave them alone. They want to get married, just be happy for them."

"Are we already arguing?"

Lana turned her attention toward the dining room opening, where Tate Wentworth came strutting through. The boy might be young, but Lana thought he looked just like his big half-brother. Carson did have a special relationship with Tate. During their debates and the campaign, Tate seemed to be his biggest supporter.

"We are done arguing," Carson stated. "Have a seat. We're just getting started."

Tate took a seat across from them and Alli finished filling all the plates before she took a seat at the opposite end of the table from Hank.

"Our families have fought for a century," Hank went on. "How the hell do you think this is going to look to the rest of the Wentworths?"

Carson shook his head as he reached for his steak knife and fork. "I think it's going to look like Lana and I don't care about a feud that has nothing to do with us or our future. It's going to look like our love will bridge the families together and anyone that doesn't want to get on board with that is too busy living in the past. And that's not my problem."

Lana swallowed the lump in her throat. How did Carson do this? How did he just spout off exactly what needed to be said, and at precisely the right time? Perhaps that's how he'd defeated her for the presidency.

"Harmon wants this feud to die down, so this is serendipitous," Alli stated. "Let's focus on the happy and that these two are ready to start their lives together without the black cloud of a family war hanging over their heads. So tell me what your plans are so far for the wedding?"

Lana glanced down the table at Alli's questioning, eager gaze. "Well, I don't have anything finalized quite yet. This is all so new."

"I'm sure you have something in mind," Alli replied. "Most women have an idea of a dream wedding. A favorite color or a favorite flower. What about the ring?"

Lana held up her hand and flashed the still foreign object.

"Oh, Carson," Alli gasped. "You did good. I love it."

"She deserves something just as striking and bold as she is," he told his stepmother.

Lana placed her hand back in her lap and stared at her plate of food. There was no way she could eat all of this…not with all the nerves in her belly.

"Do you want outside or in?" Alli asked. "Hank and I had an outdoor fall wedding and it was absolutely beautiful."

Of course, Lana had given her real wedding some thoughts. She just hated sharing them now because she didn't want to share her personal, intimate ideas in a fake setting.

But, since she was a terrible liar, she had to stick with the truth and what she knew.

"I've always loved the idea of an outdoor wedding. Something small and intimate," she told them. "Something with just a few friends. My favorite color is blue and my favorite flower is a lily. I guess I could incorporate those things."

"You don't want a large wedding?" Hank asked.

Lana turned her attention to him and shook her head. "I'm not one to be flashy with my personal life. I know I can be over-the-top with so many other things, but something like a wedding, I'd be fine with just my fiancé and the minister, and of course a few close friends."

Hanks silver eyebrows drew together. "The Wentworths are a vast family. I'm sure there are many Langleys who would want to attend. The fact that these two families are finally coming together will bring the entire town of Royal."

Yeah, that's another reason she was so glad this was fake. The idea of all those people watching her marry made her twitchy. She did value a private life, especially one with the man she intended to spend every day with.

An intimate wedding with a grand party afterward would be just fine. Something like merging these two families would be worthy of a town celebration.

Too bad that wouldn't come to fruition.

"We can discuss the guest list later," Carson stated, coming to her rescue. "I didn't know your favorite color or favorite flower, though."

Lana smiled as she reached for her glass of wine, but Hank, of course, had to chime in.

"That's because you two are rushing into this marriage without thinking."

Oh, Lana had thought…she'd done little else since Harmon assumed they were together. But there was no way she could actually start planning anything. She wouldn't pull businesses or people in just to have to cancel things in a few weeks. If she and Carson could just keep feigning love for a month, attend the dance, and make the big announcement about the women's wing, then they could call off the engagement and still remain friends.

There. The plan was all laid out and quite logical. All of this would ultimately be for the greater good and nobody would be hurt in the end—she hoped that was her truth. The last thing she wanted was to end up pleasing everyone else, only to end up with a broken heart.

"We're not rushing," Carson argued. "And you can't talk us out of this, so move on."

"I think it's cool," Tate chimed in as he shoved

a bite of steak in his mouth. "This family-fighting thing sounds like stuff old people do. At least Lana and Carson are trying to make things right."

Lana bit the inside of her cheek to keep from smiling. She'd never really talked to Tate before. She'd seen him plenty at Carson's side, but the young man did have a valid point. Well, it would be valid if Lana and Carson were actually going to go through with the wedding.

Even though this was all for show, that didn't mean they couldn't bridge the family gap. Why not? What could be so bad that one hundred years later these families were still at each other's throats? Whatever happened in the past surely had nothing to do with the people who were here today…save for Harmon.

"Carson, how is the club going?" Alli asked. "Any new plans now that you're president?"

As much as she hated the reminder of her loss, Lana would much rather this topic than trying to come up with wedding details she didn't have and didn't plan on having.

Lana ate as much as she could with her overactive nerves, and thankfully, when the dinner was over, Carson didn't want to stick around too long. He chatted a little with Tate and then he escorted Lana from the estate and back into his SUV.

Finally, she could breathe a sigh of relief. One major milestone down in their fake engagement… and too many more to go.

Nine

"Well, that went well."

Carson headed out of the long drive, away from the estate. Lana had been quiet through most of the dinner and she still sat quiet in the passenger seat as she stared out the window.

"Did it?" she asked softly. "Because it feels like your father hates me."

"Did you want him to like you? This isn't real, you know, and your last name is still Langley. He's not going to be ready to drop this feud as quick as my great-grandfather. Dad doesn't know any different but to despise any Langley."

Something about Lana's tone and her question had him wondering if she really did care about the impression she'd make. Something about this evening had upset Lana and suddenly Carson realized he never wanted to see her upset...or be the cause of her pain.

He'd thought this temporary plan would be easy and they'd get through it together, with no one the wiser. But Carson hadn't thought about how real emotions would come into play in a fake setting.

"Forget I said anything," she stated as she shifted to face him. "I'm just tired and I definitely haven't forgotten the situation I'm in. I guess I just didn't expect so much animosity."

Carson hadn't really, either, but he should have. Even on the phone before arriving, his father had been cranky and skeptical about the whole thing. But Carson at least thought his father would have manners...which clearly hadn't been the case.

"I apologize if he made you uncomfortable."

Lana sighed and straightened in her seat. "Not for you to apologize. You didn't do anything wrong."

"Didn't I?" Carson gripped the wheel even tighter. "I could have set Harmon straight when he assumed we were together. I could have just been up-front and honest, but the last month or so he's gotten slower and more tired. He's dying. And that damn diary..."

Lana's hand rested on his thigh. "We were both in that room and I went along with it as well. Though I thought for sure you had planned that little ambush."

"Ambush?" he asked. "I swear, I was just as caught off guard as you."

"I realize that now, but at the time I was tempted to walk out and let you deal with your great-grandfather on your own."

That hand on his leg was so simple, a gesture meant to console, but all it did was get his blood pumping as he sped up just a little.

"I'm glad you didn't," he told her. "Now we're both getting what we wanted for the club and maybe with this engagement, this crazy rift will come to an end. Even when we call off the engagement, we'll have to make it seem like we realized we're better as friends, but that we're glad we could forge the families together."

There. That all sounded logical and like a simple plan that would work and everyone would still be happy in the end.

Carson drove along in silence, still very much aware that her hand was still on his thigh. Did she mean to leave it there? Did she want something more to come from this night?

A one-night stand was easy to do because there was the one night and then nothing. But now they had slept together the past two nights, so he had no clue as to the expectations on her end. Carson would gladly take another night with her, but he also didn't want to overstep or disrespect her, either.

"Tate seems like a nice young man."

Lana's statement pulled Carson from his thoughts.

"He is a great brother," he agreed. "I was a little stunned and embarrassed when Dad and Alli announced they were having a baby, but Tate has become like my best friend. We have just enough of an age gap between us that we're friends and I can give him adult advice without him feeling like I'm his dad."

"That's nice to have someone in your life like that. I don't know what I'd do without Abby. We've leaned on each other quite a bit over the years."

Carson knew Lana's brother had passed some time ago, but his widow, Abby, and Lana had remained the very best of friends. Two strong women like that were bound to create a solid bond. Abby had fought nearly ten years ago for women to be able to join the Cattleman's Club. Her hard work had tipped the hands of the board and women had been welcome members since.

Now Lana was carrying on what her sister-in-law had started and Carson couldn't fault her for fighting for those female ranchers she represented. She was the chairwoman of the TCC Women's Association. She wouldn't back down and those women were damn lucky to have someone so determined on their side.

Carson made a turn and Lana shifted, her hand suddenly sliding off his thigh.

"Where are we going?" she asked.

"I'm going to show you where I live."

"Did you want to ask me if I wanted to go?"

Carson shrugged. "Do you?"

"Depends on your intentions once you get me there."

Carson couldn't help but laugh as he gave a quick glance her way and found her smiling.

"I'd never take advantage," he assured her.

"What if I take advantage of you?"

Damn. His entire body heated with just that one question. Lana could make him want more than he ever had before. Desiring a woman was nothing new, but this aching, relentless need he had for her was becoming too all-consuming. There had never been a woman like this before. He had to chalk it up to a mind game. He knew he had to pretend to be with the public, so perhaps that's all it was. He just figured why not keep up the pretenses behind closed doors…minus the whole love part.

"Have you checked online to see if Sierra posted our story?" Lana asked.

Our story.

For the next month, everything he did would be joined with Lana. They were a team whether he wanted to be or not.

"I've been too busy," he replied. "I take it you haven't looked?"

Lana reached for her bag and pulled out her cell. The bright screen lit up the interior of his vehicle as he passed the motion sensor for his five-car garage. Up ahead, the door opened to his bay and he eased inside, amid his other rides. He had a car for each mood and occasion. These were just the everyday vehicles. Behind his home, there was another five-car garage with his antique collection and the cars that only came out for special occasions.

"Oh, wow."

Lana's gasp had him jerking toward her as he killed the engine. "What is it?" he asked. "Bad article?"

"I haven't even gotten to the article." She turned her cell to face him so he could see the photo of the two of them. "I can't get past this."

Carson stared at the image, then reached to take the phone from her hands.

TCC President and Soon-to-be First Lady in Love

If that catchy headline didn't grab a reader's attention, the romantic photograph sure as hell would. Sierra had told them she wanted pictures in his office. The photo had Lana in her killer red pencil dress hugging every damn curve as she sat on the edge of his desk with her legs crossed. Carson stood behind her, leaning forward with one hand flat on his desk next to her hip, the other on her shoulder, easing her hair away from her neck.

And the way they were staring into each other's eyes could damn near set the phone on fire. How the hell had he not noticed how she stared at him? How could he not hide his own desires?

There would be no denying their chemistry, not after everyone got wind of this. Sierra was a force and she would make sure the town knew to look at her new article…a side piece on what she was really doing here.

"Damn. We look good."

Lana laughed, just as he'd expected her to. Sex was one thing, but another tone seemed to take over this picture—there was something on display that suggested they were much more than lovers. Perhaps it was the afterglow of their evening before, but Carson was getting another tone.

Which was absurd. There was nothing more here than sex and a business agreement. He and Lana were both on the same page as far as this arrangement was concerned. They might be lying to the world, but they weren't lying to each other.

"We do," she finally agreed. "I'm turning myself on."

Now Carson laughed. She always managed to do that. Somehow she knew how to catch him off guard and say the unexpected—although by now he should realize Lana would always tell the truth and her words were always bold.

"I think that's my job." He handed her phone back to her, grazing her fingertips with his. "Let's go inside."

She cocked her head and quirked a perfectly arched eyebrow. "You mean you're not going to make out with me in the front seat of your car?"

"I'm humbled by the idea you think I'm that young, but when I have a woman, she'll be in my bed."

Lana eased back against the door. "So now I'm just any woman? You know how to make your fiancée feel special."

"You know what I mean, Lana. I'm not some innocent. You and I both had relationships before this and we'll have them after this engagement is over."

That sounded so odd, but truthful. He had to keep reminding himself of the facts or he'd get lost in this entire charade. Spending the nights with Lana could make any man lose track of the end goal. She was a powerful woman in more ways than one.

Carson exited the vehicle and went around to open her door. When he extended his hand, she peered up at him with those expressive eyes that held so many passionate promises. He'd already had her, yet he was just as anxious and revved up as their first time.

How long would it take to get her out of his system?

He'd better enjoy every minute now, because no matter what he wanted or craved, their time would be up in a month.

Lana placed her hand in his and slid out of the car, rising to lean against his body, trapping their hands between their chests.

"You talk too much," she told him. "And I don't want to discuss our past or future bedmates. I believe I was promised a tour. Let's start with your bedroom."

Carson's body stirred as he took his free hand and palmed her rounded hip. "I won't make it that far."

He crushed his mouth to hers and urged her with him as he backed to the entryway into his house. When he reached the step, he eased back from her slightly so he could turn and open the door and disarm his security system.

But he froze.

Those moist lips and heavy-lidded eyes, coupled with the flushed look on her chest and cheeks, had him nearly going back on his vow not to take her in his car. She was too damn sexy and had managed to hold her own with his father…which was really saying something.

Everything about her pulled at him in ways he'd

never imagined and they were only a few days into this farce.

He was in a hell of a predicament with this one… but Lana Langley was worth the trouble. He'd deal with the consequences later. Much later.

Ten

Lana didn't want to talk. Talking to Carson made her realize he wasn't an enemy. Talking made her realize they had more in common than she first thought. Talking made her want to uncover more about the man she should hate.

But, no, she didn't hate him. She was more fascinated than she cared to admit.

So no talking. Sex she could handle. She had to keep everything shallow and superficial so she could come out on the other side of this charade unscathed.

Great sex for a month? There was no reason to mess all of that up by getting mixed up in feelings.

But there was something on Carson's face, something she couldn't identify.

She reached around him and turned the knob, silently gesturing for him to move on in. She knew his mind was spinning and whatever his thoughts were, she didn't want to know. Anything he had to think on that long would not be good for their situation.

Passion was easy and passion was all she wanted.

Carson turned, stepped into the house, punched in a code, and reached for her hand to pull her on inside as well. Lana closed the door behind her and immediately reached for the zipper behind her back. When her pencil dress spread apart down her spine, she shrugged her arms until the material fell down to her waist.

There it was. Carson was back in the moment and out of his internal thoughts, which had pulled him away moments ago. His eyes widened as they landed on her bright blue demi bra. That look he gave her each time he saw her bare only boosted her confidence.

"When you look at me like that..."

She didn't mean to say anything, so she stopped. She didn't want to talk, right? No feelings. No emotions. There was no room for any of that here.

"What?" he asked. "What were you going to say?"

Lana shook her head, but Carson reached for

her. He slid his thumbs in the dress and pushed the piece the rest of the way down to puddle at her feet.

"When I look at you I see beauty," he told her. "When I look at you I see a strong woman who challenges me and makes me realize this fake engagement isn't such a bad idea. I see a woman who is just as determined as I am and I see a woman I can't get enough of."

He saw too much. He used words that made her uncomfortable because she couldn't let this temporary situation get out of control. She had a goal—*they* had a goal.

Lana stepped out of her pooled dress and did a seductive little spin to keep his mind on the sex and less on their forced predicament.

He cursed beneath his breath, then reached for her. She'd barely gotten back around before he gripped her backside, pulled her against him, and lifted her up. Lana locked her ankles behind his back, and her heels clanked to the hardwood floor in the process.

"You're driving me out of my mind," he muttered against her mouth as he carried her through the house. "If I'd known what you were wearing beneath that dress, we would have never made it to dinner."

"I would have been fine with that," she told him. "I'd rather be alone."

He reached the base of a grand staircase that

curved toward a wide landing before going up to the second floor. She'd have to admire the rest of his house later—she had a need for something other than impressive interior design right now.

"Stay the night."

Lana eased back and stared into his dark eyes.

"Stay," he repeated. "I'll take you home tomorrow. I'm not looking for anything more than what we agreed on. I just want you to myself all night."

He'd stayed at her house most of the night the last two nights, but he'd been gone before morning on both occasions. This was different. She was going into this knowing she'd stay in his bed and they'd wake up in the morning…like a real relationship.

"Carson—"

"Nothing more, Lana." He nipped at her lips and started up the steps. "I want you in my bed and I'm not ready to let you go yet."

Yet. At least he knew he would be letting her go.

She rested her head against the crook in his shoulder. "I'll stay."

Maybe she was making a mistake, but she'd made them before. At least she knew what all of this was for—she knew exactly what she needed to do and not do. Her eyes were wide open here and she was in charge.

And right now, she was going to take what Carson was offering. A night of passion with a man who made her toes curl and pleasured her in ways she'd never known was an obvious yes.

Once they reached the landing, Carson continued carrying her until she found herself between the wall and his rock-hard body. She lifted her head to look into his eyes, only to find him using the wall to keep her held in place while he worked on his pants.

"Do you have protection?" she asked.

He froze. "Upstairs in my room."

That seemed so far away right now. The indescribable need had her speaking before really thinking.

"I'm on birth control and I'm clean," she told him. "It's your call."

That muscle in his jaw clenched as his lips thinned. "I'm clean, but are you sure?"

Lana nodded, realizing she was sure. This was all so rushed, so temporary, but she wanted to feel him with no boundaries. Maybe that was crossing the line she swore she wouldn't cross, but this wasn't emotional, right? This was still that raw, physical need. Her heart certainly wasn't involved in this moment.

"I'm sure," she told him.

Lana braced her hands on his shoulders and waited. Carson finished getting his pants out of the way before he met her gaze. That intense stare locked her in place, and when he joined their bodies, Lana couldn't help but close her eyes and let her head fall back as she arched into his touch… into the sensations that overcame her.

This was their third night together and Lana still had those giddy feelings just like the first.

Carson set a fast, frantic pace that had her body climbing higher and higher. She cried out his name and was near the point of begging when his mouth closed over the curve in her neck, which only sent her body over the edge. She rocked her hips against his, using the wall at her back as leverage to complete her satiating experience.

Carson pumped harder and trembled as his mouth traveled from her neck up to her lips. He kissed her with a fierce passion she'd only come to fully know from this man. Never before had someone thoroughly loved her like Carson.

But love wasn't involved here…not in the sex and not in the engagement.

Lana pulled in a deep breath as her body started to settle. Carson grazed his damp lips across hers then rested his forehead to hers. His warm breath fell on her heated skin and she closed her eyes, wondering if she'd be able to just walk away from this unscathed. She was only a few days in and she had way too many to go…which meant she'd better guard her heart, or she'd find herself falling for the enemy.

Eleven

Carson scrolled through the numerous spreadsheets Lana had sent him last week. Had that already been a week ago? His life had certainly taken quite the turn. He'd not only found himself "engaged," but he'd also found himself bed-hopping between Lana's place and his. There wasn't a night they hadn't spent together and there seemed to just be some unspoken agreement that they'd use each other as some physical outlet during this crazy time.

The numbers before him seemed to all blur and run together as his mind flooded with images of his new sexy lover. How the hell was he supposed to concentrate on anything during the day when he could only count down to the evenings?

A tap on his door had him shifting from his computer screen to the opening of his office door.

"Hey."

Tate came in and took a seat across from Carson. The solemn look on the boy's face had Carson immediately shifting from his own thoughts to what was bothering his brother.

"What's up?" Carson asked, resting his elbows on his desk.

"Just wanted to come by and see how things were going."

Carson shook his head. "I know you too well. What's really going on? Still girl trouble?"

Tate sighed and shrugged. "Why are they so complicated?"

Carson couldn't help but laugh. "It's not so much that they are complicated, you just have to figure out a way to make your complicated and their complicated work together…if that makes sense."

Tate's questioning gaze landed on Carson. "Is that what happened with you and Lana? Because you two were really at each other during the campaign. I never would have thought you two would have ended up together. And engaged? Dude, that was fast."

Yeah, Carson's head was still spinning, but he couldn't let anyone in on this secret…not even Tate.

"Sometimes things just click into place," he replied, which was the truth. "Lana is headstrong and determined, which are qualities I respect and definitely understand. We have the same drive for business and have similar life goals."

"She's pretty hot, too," Tate said with that teen smirk he had.

Carson nodded. "Any man would be blind not to notice how attractive she is. We definitely have our differences, no doubt about that, and our families have been at odds for decades, but sometimes you just have to power through and go after what you want."

That was all damn good advice. Maybe if he actually loved Lana, he could stand behind these words. Tate didn't need to know the predicament Carson had gotten himself into—the teen just needed basic advice.

"Do you really like this girl?" Carson asked. "Carly, right?"

Tate nodded. "I like her, but she doesn't get me. She's not into the ranch life and that's all I know and love."

"Have you invited her to the ranch?" Carson asked. "Maybe try to show her your life and then do something that she loves in return. Relationships aren't fifty-fifty. You really have to give one hundred percent of yourself and so does she."

Man, the more he talked, the better he was sounding. Truth was, he knew nothing of relationships. His friends Drake and Cammie were completely in love, as were Jackson and Haley, and Gabe and Ros. Actually, many of his friends and fellow TCC members had fallen in love and married recently. There was definitely something in the air around here, but nothing he wanted to be a part of.

"I had her at the house for dinner a couple times," Tate told him. "We've never taken any horses out into the fields or anything."

"Well, there you go." Carson smiled. "Invite her for a horseback ride, show her what you love about the ranch without arguing or seeing all your differences."

Tate nodded. "That's a good idea."

"I'm full of good ideas. All you have to do is listen."

Tate got to his feet, shoved his hands in his denim pockets and stared more intently than before.

"Think you and Lana will have kids?" Tate asked.

Carson's breath caught. Kids were certainly not something he'd given any thought to with Lana. Hell, they went from enemies to being engaged so damn fast, his head was still spinning.

"Let's just get down the aisle before you worry about us having kids," Carson joked as he got to his feet. "Why don't you call your girl and then let me know how your date goes? If you really want to be romantic, you can always have the chef prepare a nice picnic that you could take out by the pond."

"Thanks, man."

"Anytime."

Tate turned and started toward the door, but stopped and glanced over his shoulder. "Do you care that dad thinks this marriage is a bad idea?"

Even if his engagement to Lana had been authentic, he wouldn't care what his father thought. Yes, he'd want his dad on board with the next chapter in his life, but on the other hand a Langley-Wentworth union could actually solidify this generation and pave the way for the next and all of them thereafter.

"Dad will come around," Carson replied. "Don't worry about me."

Tate gave him that signature Wentworth cocky grin. "Does anything ever bother you?"

The woman who drove him crazy both in bed and out, and in totally opposite ways, but that tidbit wasn't something worth sharing with his teen brother.

"Plenty, but I can't let it bother me or get in the way of my goals. And that's advice for anything from your personal to your professional life. If you want something, don't let anything stand in your way."

Tate gave a final nod before he left the office, leaving Carson hoping he had given him the best advice possible. The silence surrounding him also left him wondering who the hell was going to give him advice, because he needed to know how to maneuver through this delicate situation with his new fiancée.

* * *

"Let me get all of this straight."

Lana didn't like that tone from Abby. Lana also didn't like lying to her best friend and sister-in-law, but right now she didn't have a choice.

"I'm still getting used to you being engaged to Carson Wentworth, and now you're wanting my help to throw your engagement party at the end of the month?"

Lana smiled as she crossed her legs on the sofa in her office at the clubhouse. No matter that her insides were swirling with nerves and anxiety—she couldn't let any of that show on the outside.

"Pretty much," Lana confirmed. "I can do a low-key wedding, but an engagement party should be extravagant and fun. Something over-the-top and not near as intimate as the actual wedding."

Abby laughed and tucked her vibrant red hair behind her ears. "Lana, this is insane. You hate Carson. You hate all the Wentworths, actually."

"I don't, though. I was just brought up to hate that family simply for their name," Lana explained, glad she could at least tell some truth here. "I never really dealt too much with Carson until the campaign and, of course, he wasn't my favorite because he was my opponent."

The still skeptical Abby narrowed her eyes and tipped her head. Lana knew that look—Abby wasn't buying this story, but Lana had to stay on the path she'd started. She still couldn't believe she'd forged such a secret bond with Carson, of all people in this world.

"I'm just trying to figure out where all of this came from and why it's moving so fast."

Fast? If only Abby knew. Every bit of Lana wanted to just spill every detail—get it off her chest and out in the open. Lana desperately wanted some sound advice from her very best friend.

"You, of all people, have to understand where I'm coming from. You fell for your opponent, too."

"Oh, I'm well aware," Abby agreed with a smile.

But that smile eased away and skepticism fell back into place as Abby continued to stare and wait for answers.

Lana knew that Abby would be a tough sell because nobody knew her like Abby. They were just as tight as biological sisters and shared everything. So during the campaign days, Abby had heard Lana's ranting and hatred for Carson on the daily.

And now Lana had to sell a marriage to the man.

Uneasy and anxious, Lana got to her feet and crossed to the little minibar area she kept on the wall behind her desk. She didn't have a big office, certainly nothing like the president, but she did have her own space, since she was the main woman to get things done for the female ranchers in the area.

Despite wanting a larger office, Lana had made do with what she had and had accessorized the hell

out of the space with a plush white love seat, blush
throw pillows, a white desk with a white-and-gold
accent chair, and the chandelier she'd had sent from
an online boutique in LA. She might be a country
girl at heart, but she had all the taste of the big-
city bling.

"Chardonnay?" Lana asked, holding up a stem-
less wineglass.

"I'm going to need the entire bottle from the way
this conversation is going."

Lana laughed as she poured two glasses and
crossed back over the white faux-fur rug. She
handed Abby her drink and then took a seat, once
again crossing her legs and ready to tackle this
topic.

"You've not only found love once, but twice,"
Lana began. "When it's real, there's not much you
can do to stop it."

Ugh. She was lying—she wasn't doing the best
job, but she was doing it. Abby knew her better than
anyone, and if Lana could put this over on her, then
there would be no problem posing as an imposter
to the rest of the town.

"I just don't believe it." Abby took a sip of her
drink and swirled the contents before taking another sip. "Don't get me wrong, Carson is a damn
fine man to look at, but he's so arrogant."

Oh, there was no arguing that fact, but for reasons Lana couldn't explain, his arrogance seemed

to be growing on her. In the bedroom, that arrogance turned into something downright sexy and irresistible.

"He's determined," Lana amended. "I believe that's one of the qualities you love about me, yes?"

Abby rolled her eyes. "I love you no matter what. And I don't want to be a black cloud over your happiness. So if this is what you want, then I'm all for it. I just don't want you hurt."

Well, that made two of them, but so far, so good. Nights filled with passion and days filled with meetings and party planning weren't the worst ways to spend her time.

"So you'll help me plan the engagement party?" Lana asked.

"You know I will." Abby shifted on the sofa and rested her elbow on the back as a wide smile spread across her face. "What are you thinking? Do you want to keep the rustic vibe going, like the clubhouse? I mean, I assume you're holding the event here."

"I am, but I'm not sure about rustic. I want a good mix of both our tastes."

"So let's start with Carson, because I know you as well as I know myself. What are his tastes?"

"He loves the color green, he loves his family, he's a night owl, and he'd do anything to make me happy."

Lana couldn't help but smile as images of their

nights together flooded her mind. Keeping her happy was definitely first and foremost in his mind when they were alone. She'd never had such a giving lover, or a man who knew exactly what to do without a single word.

Why did he have to be so perfectly imperfect for her?

"Well, that grin on your face is rather telling," Abby teased. "But I don't think those kind of details are the ones we can incorporate into the party."

Lana shifted her focus back to her drink and took a sip. She hadn't even realized she'd been grinning while thoughts of Carson rolled through her mind.

Damn it. She was getting in far deeper than she'd ever intended or envisioned.

This party clearly had to be about the engagement and the big announcement regarding the funds from Harmon. She had to keep her mind and her focus on those goals, because her emotions, or any type of newfound feelings for Carson, had no place in this faux engagement.

And that funding part was a secret Lana was keeping from Abby as well. If Lana let that slip, Abby would know full well this engagement was not legit.

Too many lies. Too much like her father. For all these years, Lana had vowed not to be like her mother, but she'd gone and done the opposite.

"What about keeping things simple?" Abby suggested. "I know you are completely over-the-top with nearly everything from your clothes to your decor. But hear me out. What if you just had simple centerpieces? They can still make a statement, but in more of a fun way. I've seen people have mini-cakes on each table, a different flavor and style even would be interesting. Do you know a color scheme? Obviously green if that's what Carson likes."

"What about a classic green with a pale gold? Something to soften the shade?" Lana suggested.

"I love it." Abby set her glass on the table in front of the love seat and pulled her phone from her bag. "I'm taking notes now. This is so exciting. I love planning parties with other people's money."

"That's why you're perfect for this job, because I'm working with Carson on renovation ideas for a whole new women's wing."

Abby's eyebrows rose. "Is that so?"

"It took some persuasion, but he's on board. I can't wait to make an official announcement, so don't say anything just yet."

Abby beamed. "I'm so proud of the hard work you're putting into the club. I never imagined it would grow like it has when I first petitioned for female members."

"You were definitely a pioneer," Lana acknowledged. "I'm just making sure we get our own designated space. I think something more feminine will be perfect. I imagine baby showers and bridal showers and maybe even monthly wine-and-dine events. Something just for us. I'll work out the details for all of that later, I'm just starting on the design and getting a contractor and budget finalized."

Abby reached over and squeezed Lana's hand. "This is so exciting. You seem so happy and I guess I have Carson to thank for that. I guess this will make you the first lady?"

The first lady? That wasn't the title she wanted. She'd wanted president, but that wasn't to be.

And as far as thanking Carson for her sudden happiness? Maybe he was partially responsible. He did make her smile, and he had become a delicious distraction, but all of this was temporary and nothing was real.

The fact that the only person she could be "real" with right now was the man she was in a fake-committed relationship with was so ironic and completely unfair. None of this made sense, but she only had three more weeks to go.

Now, if she could just keep her heart guarded that long, she'd come out on the other side unscathed.

Twelve

Carson watched Lana smooth her hair over one shoulder, then shift her stance. She blew out a breath, and then adjusted her hair once more.

"Stop fidgeting," Carson muttered. "You look as beautiful as ever."

She glanced over at him as they stood on the porch of Cammie and Drake's home. He hadn't even knocked yet, but something had Lana behaving like a ball of nerves.

"What's wrong?" he asked, turning to face her fully.

She closed her eyes and shook her head. "It's just so real, yet not, if that makes sense. We're lying to everyone around us and I'm actually planning an engagement party like this is going to happen. Will we just be hated when we call this off?"

Carson took her hands in his and offered what he hoped was a reassuring squeeze. That fierce look in her eyes hid the vulnerability, but he saw it there. Maybe some people wouldn't recognize her anxiety, but he'd come to know her pretty well in their last week and a half together. Intimacy really did pull out a whole other side to someone, and he'd not only gotten physically intimate with her, but they'd also connected on an intellectual level.

"Nobody will hate us," he assured her. "Don't lose sight as to why we started this. Harmon's dying wish and to have the funds for the club. We are doing good for so many people. I'm right here with you, Lana. I won't let you fall."

Her eyes softened as her shoulders relaxed. She gave a slight smile and leaned forward, pressing her lips to the corner of his mouth.

He wanted more. Every time he touched her, no matter how innocent, he wanted more.

But at the same time, he also wanted her to realize that she wasn't in this by herself. Hell, he was the one who'd gotten her in this mess, so if she fell, he'd certainly be there to catch her. No matter what happened at the end of all of this, he would do anything to prevent her from getting hurt.

In such a short time, Carson had come to care

about Lana. Great sex aside, he did respect and value her as a confidante and a formidable adversary. Never in his life did he believe his closest friend and lover would be a Langley.

Yes, this was all temporary, he totally understood that. But there was no way once this engagement was over that they could—or would—go back to being enemies.

The door swung open, immediately followed by the sound of someone clapping.

"You two lovebirds are adorable."

Carson kept hold of Lana's hands as he shifted his attention to Cammie.

"I was just stealing a moment with my girl," he stated.

"Which is what makes you two so cute," Cammie added, her smile wide. "Come on in. I'm so thrilled to have you guys here. Drake is just getting Micah changed for the third time today. Diaper blowouts—you don't want any more information than that."

Carson laughed. "No, I don't."

He gestured for Lana to go in ahead of him. Once they were inside the spacious ranch home, Cammie closed the door behind them and a moment later Drake came down the hall with Micah in his arms.

"Hey, guys." Drake came over and kissed Lana on the cheek before turning to Carson and shaking his hand. "This is great that you two could come by. Cammie has been dying to know all the details of the engagement since she read about it."

Lana stiffened beside him, but he slid his thumb in an easy pattern over the back of her hand. He'd give her credit, though—she kept that megawatt smile in place.

"It was sort of a whirlwind," Carson admitted. "But definitely worth it."

"Love is worth everything," Cammie replied as she reached for Micah. "Come on into the dining room. I just set everything up. I hope you all like Italian. I was craving some carbs."

"Italian and carbs are my love language," Lana chimed in. "Is there anything I can do to help you set up?"

Cammie started through the foyer and then into the dining area, cradling Micah with one arm.

"Nope. Just have a seat."

"Oh, I left the wine out in the car."

Lana started to turn, but Carson placed his hands on her shoulders. "I've got it. Go on ahead."

"You didn't need to bring wine."

He heard Cammie's statement as he stepped back onto the porch. The door closed behind him just as his cell vibrated in his pocket. He stopped and slid the phone out to check the screen and sighed.

Part of him wanted to let it go to voice mail, but the other part knew he had an obligation to his family. So he answered.

"Dad, what's up?"

"I'm visiting Granddad and I didn't know if you could come on over for a bit."

"Now isn't a good time." Carson headed toward his SUV and retrieved the bottle of cabernet. "Is something wrong?"

"No, no. Nothing like that. I was just having an interesting talk and Granddad mentioned a large sum of money going to the club."

"That's right, but people aren't supposed to know about that right now. We plan on making a surprise announcement at our engagement party at the end of the month."

"Is that why you're doing this?" his father accused.

Carson stilled. "Doing what?"

"Marrying the Langley woman."

Carson clenched his teeth and gripped the bottle of wine. "I'm marrying her because I want to and because we are in love. If you aren't happy with our reasons or if you have some hang-up, then that's your problem. I love you, Dad, but Lana is my fiancée and we're out to dinner right now, so I'll have to call you tomorrow."

He disconnected the call and pulled in a deep breath, then another, to calm his nerves before he headed back inside. The moment he stepped into the dining room, Lana turned to smile, but quickly tipped her head.

"Everything okay?" she asked, her eyebrows drawn in.

And wasn't that something. How she could pick up on his tension in just a fraction of a second absolutely floored him. Was she that in tune with his emotions and frustrations?

"Everything is fine," he assured her, leaning down to kiss her on the cheek.

Maybe the kiss was a show of their affection for Cammie and Drake, maybe the kiss was to convince her he was indeed all right, or maybe he'd kissed her because he just wanted to feel that simple touch. Odd that the very brief call with his dad had him wanting to get closer to Lana. That was something he'd have to think about later, not when he was in the midst of a dinner party hosted by great friends.

Carson circled the table and handed the bottle to Drake before going back around to take a seat next to Lana. Her leg brushed his, reminding him that he'd been at her place before this. He'd stopped by a little early, which only ended up with them in her bedroom, but not quite making it to the bed. He'd taken her right there against the wall inside the doorway.

When she'd answered the door in that damn dress with those spiky heels, he hadn't been able to resist. He still couldn't decide whether that whole girl-next-door vibe, or her killer curves in dresses, was his favorite look.

Either way, he couldn't wait to get back to her place and slide that dress up that shapely body and toss it aside. He hadn't quite taken the time he really wanted to, but now that he had her thigh against his, that only reminded him that he wasn't finished with her.

Only two and a half weeks left until they would ultimately go their separate ways...at least in their personal lives. They would still be working together in regard to the women's wing she wanted to complete.

Cammie had handed the baby off to Drake and then got all of the food ready and settled in at the table. All the while Drake started feeding Micah a bottle. The two seemed to work flawlessly with their temporary family.

"How is life with a little one?" Lana asked. "You all seem to be doing really well with him."

Cammie beamed. "He is an absolute joy to have. I've always wanted children, but Drake was more career-oriented. Micah is a wonderful influence, though, and Drake is doing really well with the adjustment. Taking care of his teenage stepsister was quite different than caring for an infant. He sees the joy there can be with children now and wouldn't change this for anything."

"He's definitely opened my eyes to future possibilities," Drake added as he rocked gently side to side while feeding the baby. "This experience might be tragic, but we are getting a good idea of how we would be as parents."

Carson reached for his wineglass. "Parenting looks good on you."

"Well, love looks good on you two." Cammie smiled across the table, her eyes darting between Carson and Lana. "Tell me all about the engagement. Your ring is absolutely stunning, by the way. But more importantly, I'm so glad we're going to finally put this Wentworth-Langley feuding in the past where it belongs."

"Thank you and I completely agree," Lana replied, as she stared down at the pearl and diamonds. "We actually had a nontraditional engagement. I asked Carson."

He couldn't help but laugh as he shook his head. "That's not exactly how it went."

She shifted in her seat and quirked an eyebrow his way. Damn that was sexy. Her attitude used to annoy him, but now he found everything about her a challenge and he never turned down an intriguing challenge.

"I believe I'm the one who got down on one knee," she reminded him.

"But I already had the ring in hand when you did that."

"Oh, man, you two are seriously made to be together," Drake laughed. "You're both so hardheaded and determined. It's no wonder you fell for each other."

That's not the first time he'd heard that and he wondered if he and Lana were just that good at convincing, or if other people saw something Carson wasn't aware of.

"So do you have any wedding details yet?" Cammie asked as she passed the bowl of fresh bread. "I love weddings. There's nothing more magical."

"I don't have wedding details yet, but I do have engagement-party plans."

Lana took a piece of bread, then set down the bowl. Were her hands shaking? Maybe she hadn't been kidding when she'd told him how much she hated lying and was terrible at it. But if he could keep this conversation on the party and not the wedding, then Lana should be just fine, because the party was a legit event that was going to happen.

"Oh, tell me all about the party," Cammie begged. "I hope it's going to be big and lavish. That just seems perfect for the two of you. You guys are the most dynamic power couple the club has ever seen."

They would be an epic power couple if this union between them was on the up-and-up. There would be no stopping him and Lana in anything they set their minds to.

But that joint venture wasn't meant to be for the long-term.

"So, when is the party?" Cammie asked.

"The end of the month," Lana replied. "You will be receiving a formal invitation in a couple of days. We plan on having it at the clubhouse in the new ballroom."

Drake shifted Micah up onto his shoulder and patted his back, immediately ridding the infant of air bubbles.

"This kid is one hell of an eater," Drake laughed. "He loves bottle time."

Carson glanced to Lana and saw that wistful look in her eyes. He'd not discussed kids with her, and why would he? It's not like this arrangement had to be taken that far. Thankfully a Wentworth-Langley baby hadn't been part of Harmon's deal.

He couldn't help but imagine what type of mother she would be. Hands on, for sure. Lana wouldn't want anyone else aiding in the raising of her child. She wouldn't be the type of parent who pawned off her baby to a nanny. She'd be the woman who put a nursery corner in her office and showed everyone exactly how multitasking worked.

An immediate image of a little girl with Lana's long, dark hair and wide, expressive eyes popped into his head. No doubt her child would be a go-getter and let nothing stand in the way of dreams and goals.

Something stirred deep in his gut and he didn't like this uncomfortable, unwanted sensation. He had no clue what had him so… Hell, he couldn't even put a label on this overwhelming emotion.

Lana's eyes went from Micah to him and she blinked, then suddenly shifted away. Whatever she'd seen in his eyes had been unwanted…and he wished like hell he knew what she'd seen.

Sure, Carson wanted children one day. He wanted to carry on the Wentworth name and have another generation to pass down the family's dynasty and legacy.

A cell chime echoed in the room and Drake immediately looked to Cammie.

"Go ahead," he told her.

Cammie offered an apologetic smile as she eased back from the table. "Excuse me. So sorry about this."

She grabbed the phone from the buffet table along the wall and stepped from the room.

"We have to take all the calls right now with Eve still recovering in rehab and with the social workers checking in." Drake took the baby and placed him in the swing next to the table and turned the device on low. "We're hoping Eve will be well enough soon to be able to be released. I know she wants to be reunited with Micah."

"How is she doing?" Lana asked.

"Last update we had she's doing really well," he replied. "I know she's very determined to get back. She wants to reconnect with that bond from her late sister."

Cammie stepped back into the room, but wasn't the smiling, bubbly woman she'd been only moments ago.

"Babe," Drake began. "What's wrong?"

"That was Officer Haley Lopez. She was calling to let me know that Eve is out of rehab now, but will require six more weeks of strenuous physical therapy."

"That's good...isn't it?" Drake asked, and Carson took note of his friend's confused tone.

"It is," Cammie replied as she took her seat on the other side of the high chair. "I just realized that now we have a deadline, and even though we've been preparing ourselves, knowing this was temporary, I hate the idea of seeing him go. He's been such a pleasure to have here."

Drake's demeanor shifted into something equally solemn as Cammie's. Carson wasn't good with comforting words. He was used to dealing with business and demands and goals. He didn't like the awkward silence that seemed to settle in the room.

"Well, you all know you have at least six weeks left," Lana offered in that upbeat tone of hers. "Micah has been the luckiest little boy to have the two of you care for him and I'm sure Eve will keep you involved in his life. She's going to be so grateful to you both."

Cammie pulled in a shaky breath and nodded. "I sure hope so. I can't imagine not seeing him grow up and reaching milestones."

"Let's not borrow worries," Drake told her. "We should enjoy our time together while we have him."

Micah let out a squeal and started crying from his swing. Drake reached for him, but Cammie stood up.

"I'll get him, you need to eat. You all go ahead. I'll just set him on my lap while we talk."

Carson watched the couple and wondered just how they would actually cope once the six weeks were over. Their temporary, life-altering arrangement would change them forever.

The parallels weren't lost on him. Without thinking, he reached beneath the table and slid his hand over Lana's thigh, giving her a gentle squeeze. His gesture had nothing at all to do with anything sexual, and everything to do with the fact that he wanted to sear every moment with her into his mind—to hold onto for the time when she was ultimately gone.

Thirteen

Lana reached for Carson's hand as he assisted her from his vehicle. They'd left their dinner party and headed back to her house in silence. She wasn't sure what had been on his mind, but she knew exactly what had been on hers.

Their time was limited. She'd known that all along, obviously. But seeing another couple facing an ending to a temporary arrangement really was like a slap in the face, and a dose of reality she needed.

The passion-filled nights would come to an end, their playful relationship in public would come to an end and the man who challenged her in the absolute best ways would come to an end.

"Hey."

She shifted her attention to his intense stare.

"You okay?" he asked.

Lana smiled. "Fine."

Carson tipped his head in that sexy, adorable way she'd come to find absolutely irresistible.

"You're a terrible liar," he told her with a grin.

"I told you that in the beginning," she reminded him. "But I seem to be doing okay where our engagement is concerned."

"You are," he agreed. "But I've gotten to know you pretty well and I can tell that you're lying."

Something warm and thrilling spread through her at his admission that he'd gotten to know her… because that meant he cared for her. He might not admit such feelings, but he did care.

So what did she do with that information? Did she call him out on it and tease? No, that's what the Lana from weeks ago would have done. Even though they were in this for the ultimate goal of money, she had to admit that she'd changed. In such a short time, he'd changed her and she wasn't even sure who she was anymore.

Her only option at this point was to be honest. Never in her life did she think she'd be opening up to her enemy, but right now there was nobody else she wanted this close to her.

"I guess just seeing them come to the realization

that their time was limited really hit me," she admitted. "It just put our situation into perspective."

When Carson merely stared at her, Lana worried she might have gone too far, or exposed a side of herself that neither of them was ready for.

"Not that I'm in love with you," she continued. "I mean, you're a great guy, and honestly, we are compatible, but when I marry, I want to be completely head over heels and I want my guy to put me first in all things. I want to know I'm it for him."

"You deserve nothing less," Carson told her. "And he'll be a lucky man to have you by his side."

Lana was taken aback a bit. "You really think so? Because some men might think I'm too much to handle."

"Then they are missing out." Carson reached up, framed her face, and stared into her eyes. "Any man that doesn't want a strong, independent woman at his side is a damn fool."

There went those flutterings once again in her belly. Getting overly infatuated with Carson was a big no-no.

Why did the wrong man have all the right words?

"Can I put you down as a reference when the time comes?" she joked, desperately needing to keep things light between them.

Carson's lips quirked into a grin…which did nothing to help that curl of arousal inside her. Why did he have such control over her emotions when she'd told herself over and over to hold tight to her control?

Lana already despised the woman that would eventually come into his life. Jealousy had no place here, but Lana couldn't help the immediate reaction to the faceless lady who would step into Lana's role one day.

And that was it, wasn't it? All of this was a role. Short-term, fake, completely made up of lies and deceit—was there anything about any of that that appealed to her? And what good relationship could come from this situation? There was no real-life happily-ever-after—not for the two of them to actually end up together.

"I'm not discussing another man in your life as long as I'm the one in it." Carson's hands slid down over her shoulders and settled into the dip of her waist. He yanked her body against his. "And you're mine for the next few weeks."

His. She really shouldn't like the sound of that, but she did. Wasn't she supposed to be the strong, independent woman he'd mentioned? The deeper she fell with Carson, the more she wondered if she'd lost control somewhere.

Was she losing part of herself by getting wrapped up in all of this charade? Because that's what worried her most.

No, what worried her most was falling for Carson. That would be a complete disaster. His father was not on board with this and they were much too hardheaded to make this any longer than a month. Great sex helped to gloss over all of the anxiety and worry that kept flooding her mind. Carson was definitely good at distracting her.

"I can hear your mind working," he said, laughing. "I'm clearly not doing a good job here."

Lana placed her hands on his shoulders and tipped her head. "And here I was just thinking what a perfect distraction you were for everything going on."

"We're good for distracting each other." He leaned forward, feathering his lips over hers. "I'm about a second away from peeling you out of this dress right here in your driveway."

Just like she'd thought earlier...he had all the right words. Every word, every look, every touch held a promise of so much more to come.

"We'd better get inside," she told him, taking his hand and leading him up the brick steps to her porch.

As she glanced back, thunder rolled through the sky. Something about that ominous sound had her shivering, and not in the turned-on manner she'd become accustomed to. Between the reality hitting her hard from the dinner earlier and the storm brewing, she wanted to get inside and lock out any negativity or evil that could harm her or Carson. She had come to care for him—it would be impossible not to. But she had another sinking feeling that she might be falling for her enemy…no matter how many times she told herself that was a mistake.

And she still had over two weeks before letting him go for good.

Something had shifted. The light in Lana's eyes dimmed just enough for Carson to worry and wonder what was plaguing her mind, and what she was keeping bottled up inside. He wanted her to open up to him, to let him know what bothered her so he could fix any and all issues that bothered her. Never before had he wanted to wrap a woman in his protective embrace and slay anything that threatened her happiness.

And she would absolutely hate that he wanted to protect her. He knew full well that she could do everything herself, but she shouldn't have to. She deserved a man who would do anything she wanted, a man who would keep that smile on her face and that light shining in her eyes.

But he wasn't to be that man and he was an absolute fool for having such thoughts.

Carson took her key from her and opened her door before he said something he might regret… like opening up about these unwanted, confusing feelings.

Sex. That's what they came back for and that's what they both seemed to understand.

Lana closed the door behind him. She went to

the security panel and typed in her code, the quick succession of beeps echoing through the dark foyer.

Then she turned to face him and the accent lamp on the table lit up her face, and he saw that raw passion staring back at him. She didn't even need to say a word and he already knew what she needed. She needed him, and if she wanted to use him to forget everything, then he was more than ready to oblige.

"Is there more going on here?"

Her question sliced through his thoughts. He didn't want to assume he knew where her thought process was heading, but he had a pretty good idea. They'd been dancing around this for days. And by *this*, he meant the extra tension and unspoken emotions that had been swirling around them, pulling them closer and closer with each passing moment.

"More?" he asked.

"More than sex," she elaborated. "It just seems like for two people who were trained up to be enemies, we have a great deal in common, and other than the campaign, we haven't even bickered at each other."

"And why is that?"

Carson wasn't ready to admit anything and this might be one area he was more than willing to relinquish control. He definitely wanted to know what was in her head before he made any type of statement.

Maybe he was cut out for politics after all.

"I'd say because we think for ourselves." She

smiled and crossed her arms. "Neither one of us like to be told what to do, so the fact we're getting along, now that we're getting married, really just shows everyone how strong and determined we are."

Lana let out a soft laugh that tightened his gut and added another burst of arousal.

"I mean if we were actually getting married," she stated. "Can you imagine how crazy we would drive each other?"

Oh, he could imagine. She already drove him crazy on a daily basis…but in the most amazing of ways. He definitely couldn't admit that.

"I just don't want to get too swept up in the lies and start believing them myself."

Her smile faded and for the first time in this whole process, he saw a sliver of fear. These emotions were much too close to falling over into vulnerability and discomfort, which was something he had vowed not to let her experience.

Carson took a step forward, then another, closing the gap between them. He slid his hands up and over her shoulders, mimicking their stance from the driveway, but suddenly they'd gone from flirty and sexy to compassionate and caring.

"We're not getting swept up in anything," he assured her. "We're doing something to help the club, to help give Harmon peace of mind before he passes, and to prove our families can get along from here on out. We're breaking this toxic cycle."

He gave a gentle squeeze to her shoulders and rested his forehead against hers.

"The fact that we're involved intimately is just for us," he whispered. "Nothing says we can't take what we both want without the guilt."

"And when all of this is over…"

Yeah, that was the part he was hoping to avoid. He didn't want to think of the time when he had to let her go and go back to dating random women. He'd gotten comfortable with Lana, maybe too comfortable, too fast, but he chalked it up to the fact he knew this wasn't permanent, so why should he get comfortable? There were no consequences here and nothing actually tying him down.

Carson didn't want to talk anymore, he didn't want to analyze his future or the feelings. He wanted to make her forget any worry or doubts. Their time together was too short to allow in any negativity, and if he had to help her overcome this small hurdle she couldn't get over on her own, then that's what he'd do.

They were a team, right? At least for the time being.

Lana lifted her head slightly, silently inviting him to kiss her. Clearly, she was done talking and worrying, too. How could they speak the same language without saying a word to each other?

He reached around her back and eased down the zipper. The material parted as he grazed his fingertips over her bare skin. The second she shivered beneath his touch, Carson peeled the dress from her arms and down her body, letting it glide effortlessly to the floor.

"Carson—"

He placed a fingertip over her lips, stared into those expressive eyes, and eased back slightly.

"Just let me show you," he murmured, sliding his fingertip from her lips down her neck and to the valley between her breasts.

"Show me what?" she asked.

"Everything."

Carson lifted her and headed toward the staircase, wondering if he'd ever tire of carrying her up these steps. He wanted her in her bed, and he wanted to take his time. Every moment they'd been alone had been frantic and rushed. A woman like Lana deserved more than a few passion-filled moments. She deserved the entire night, she deserved...

A lifetime.

No. That couldn't be. There was no lifetime of them together and he wasn't even supposed to have those thoughts in his head. This situation and arrangement didn't have to be complicated.

Lana's head rested against his shoulder and something turned over in his chest. That simple, delicate gesture stemmed from nothing but trust. He'd never thought about a woman's trust before—it had never really mattered, apparently.

For reasons he didn't want to get into, Carson blocked any further emotion from entering this moment. All that mattered now was Lana. Even though they were both getting what they wanted for the club out of this situation, she'd ultimately agreed to this because of his great-grandfather.

Lana might be hard, strong, always showing her steely exterior, but there was a side to her that he liked to think only he knew. There was a side she kept hidden from the public, and she tried to hide from him, but he knew her little quirks and he knew she was fighting so hard to keep her emotions close to her chest.

Carson reached the double doors to her bedroom and used his toe to push them open. The darkened room only had a slash of moonlight falling across the bottom edge of the bed. He couldn't wait to mess up those perfectly placed blankets.

Lana's fingertips threaded through his hair at the nape of his neck. Her delicate touch never failed to turn him on. Everything about her made him want her more, from her touch to her quick banter.

This woman was the real deal. She might not give up all of her emotions, but she'd been right in admitting she couldn't lie. There was a sensitivity to her that she never showed and if he hadn't been so in tune with reading her body language and those expressive eyes, she would have fooled him into believing everything was just fine.

There was one emotion she couldn't hide, though. Desire.

Lana had to be the most passionate woman he'd ever known and in this short time, he'd come to value her even more. He found himself wanting to please her, wanting to uncover more layers to get to know her even better.

Carson crossed the dimly lit room and gently placed her on the bed. As she lay there completely bare—she hadn't worn anything under her dress— she stared up at him, and that clench in his chest happened once again.

He couldn't put a label on that and thinking too much on anything more than physical scared the hell out of him.

With her wide eyes locked on him, Carson shed himself of every piece of clothing. He reached for her foot, running his thumb along the arch. He grabbed her other foot and did the same before bending her knees and placing her feet flat on the bed.

There was never a more beautiful sight than Lana splayed out before him.

"I'm staying all night."

A wide smile spread across her face as she reached up for him. "I hadn't planned on letting you leave."

He didn't know if she meant for tonight…or at the end of the month.

Fourteen

A week of pretty much spending all of his time at Lana's home had led Carson to believe that they were even more compatible than he'd first thought. He knew they meshed in nearly all areas, but the longer he stayed, the more he wanted to.

Which was why he was back in his home. Wanting too much from Lana and this "relationship" could be detrimental to the entire process. They'd made a deal, a verbally binding agreement for a month. Nothing more.

They just needed to secure the funds from Harmon, end the feud between the Wentworths and the Langleys and move on with club business. Then they could each move on in their private lives as well.

But moving on didn't seem as exciting as it once had, and as their end date grew closer, there was a new level of anxiety he hadn't experienced before... and he wasn't quite sure what to make of it.

He needed to clear his mind a bit and circle back to focus on why he was in this position. Besides, they were a little over a week from the engagement party and that really narrowed the gap in bringing this fake engagement to an end.

Carson made his way upstairs toward his bedroom. He just wanted a shower and to do a few things before he went to see his father later. He'd not spoken to him since the phone call that interrupted Cammie and Drake's dinner party and he wanted to check in.

He told Lana he'd get in touch with her later. He wasn't sure if he should go to her house, or if he should start putting that gap between them. They were falling into an easy pattern that couldn't become the norm.

Stripping out of his clothes, he started heading toward his en suite. As he passed by his bed, something seemed off. He did a double take at his nightstand and noticed Arielle Martin's diary had been moved. It wasn't in the same spot he kept it.

Since Sierra had loaned it to him, the diary always sat beneath another book he'd been reading, but now the diary was on top and the stack had shifted.

Carson picked up the diary, then scanned through Arielle's words where she interviewed Harmon. The ragged edge from one section gave him pause.

What the hell was this? He looked closer and realized pages had been torn out. The diary had been completely intact when he'd last looked inside… which was before he went to Lana's yesterday.

Who the hell had been in his home and messed with the diary? Or had pages just been loose that he hadn't noticed? Maybe they'd slipped out.

He checked beneath the bed, in case the pages had fallen there, and he even looked in the top drawer of his nightstand. Where the hell had those pages gone? Someone had to have come in and taken them. What was on those pages that was so important?

Carson sank down on the edge of his bed and raked his hand through his hair. He hadn't seen one single thing out of place or missing other than those pages. How the hell could anyone get into his house with all the security?

It had to be someone who knew him, someone who came and went freely…someone Carson trusted to be here.

His first thought was Lana, but he really didn't believe she'd take it. Would she? Who else had been here? He certainly hadn't invited anyone else.

The thoughts weighed heavy on his mind as he went to grab a shower. He had to find out what happened to those pages and he had to figure out who the hell took them…and why.

"This party is going to be the most amazing event this club has ever seen."

Lana laughed as Abby gushed over the engagement party. Lana had asked her best friend to meet her in the ballroom so they could finalize some of the plans. She couldn't believe that in just over a week, this engagement would come and go like a wrinkle in her path of life. She and Carson would have to go back to their regularly scheduled days, and act as if they hadn't turned each other's worlds upside down and inside out.

She honestly had no clue how she was supposed to jump into the dating scene and not compare any man to Carson Wentworth.

"Well, if this is the event of the year, then it's all because you helped," Lana stated. "One thing is for sure—the night will be memorable."

As if this entire month hadn't been memorable? Lana had squeezed in years of memories with Carson in such a short time. No doubt the engagement party would also be a night she'd never forget. It was all the events that would follow that Lana wasn't looking forward to.

"I think we have everything down here," Abby stated as she did a slow turn, as if she was already seeing the space fully decorated. "Can you think of anything else we're missing?"

An actual engaged couple?

"I'm confident we've covered all the bases," Lana replied. "Do you want to see my ideas for the new women's area?"

Abby clasped her hands and let out a little squeal. "You know I do."

"Follow me." Lana gestured toward the hallway and led Abby toward her back office. "Now, nothing is finalized, Carson and I have been busy doing other things, but I'm thrilled with the vision."

"I imagine being engaged to a sexy man and planning to take over the world is time-consuming."

Lana laughed as she unlocked her office door and flipped on the light. "We're not taking over the world, but perhaps just the clubhouse."

"Well, with the way you gush when talking about him, I'm not sure how you two get anything done."

Lana paused and turned to face her best friend. "I don't gush."

Abby snickered. "Oh, girl. You most definitely gush. You mention his name and your face gets this pretty pink tint, your voice changes just a bit, and you smile like nothing I've seen before."

"What do you mean?"

What did Abby see? Obviously too much, but Lana had no clue she was giving off anything other than fake vibes. But if Abby was picking up all of that, what did that say about Lana's true feelings?

The feelings she didn't want to face. She knew they were there, under the surface. She hadn't wanted to admit it, she hadn't wanted to face the truth. But now that Abby had called her out...

"I'm just saying I'm really glad you're happy," Abby replied. "It shows and I just hope you two are always in this state."

Oh, they'd be happy once the farce came to an end. Then they could stop the public affection—but she didn't know if she wanted to. She wasn't even going to bother lying to herself at this point. She'd miss Carson's touch, his kisses...their nights together. That had nothing to do with a fake engagement and everything to do with their bond they'd formed.

When she'd tried to call him on it and bring it out in the open the night of Cammie's dinner party, the question had been somewhat dodged—in true president mode—and they'd ended up in bed. But that night there had been a shift between them, a shift that had almost brought them even closer together.

"We'll be happy," Lana assured her.

They'd be apart, but they'd create their own happiness. They were too much alike to stay together long-term, or at least that's what Lana kept telling herself. Even if they buried the feud, would that dark cloud still hover around them?

She didn't know how they could make things work, not with both of them having that type A personality. They'd get along for a while, but what happened when a problem hit them head on? What happened when they wanted to approach something major but had a difference of opinion?

That Wentworth-Langley battle mode would come back into play and Lana didn't want to risk hating him again. She liked where they were, but moving in the direction of a fully committed relationship wasn't the smartest move.

"I was hoping to run these plans by you and get your input." Lana circled back around to the original topic and moved to her desk to fire up her computer. "I think you are going to love them, but since you are the pioneer of the women's membership, I definitely want to know if you think I've missed anything."

"I'm sure you thought of all the perfect elements to add in," Abby assured her.

Lana took her laptop to the sofa and settled in beside Abby. She opened the file and started scrolling through, pointing out various upgrades, new amenities, and special perks for members only.

Abby beamed. "You nailed it. I can't believe how detailed this is, Lana. The women are going to absolutely love this."

"That's my goal."

"Is all of this in the budget?" Abby asked. "It seems rather over-the-top, even for the club."

"It's all in the budget." Just as soon as this engagement party was over and Harmon released the funds. "I've gotten bids and they are all similar, but Carson is making the final call on that."

Abby tapped on the screen a few more times, going back through the mock-up images. "These are all just so amazing. I can't wait to see it brought to life. You, my friend, are a genius."

Lana shrugged. "I don't know about that, but I do know what I like and I can't help but have expensive taste."

"That's nothing to apologize for," Abby added. "I love that you are a bold woman who knows what she wants and doesn't defend herself for it. That's why we're such good friends, even stronger than family."

Yeah, well, Lana didn't feel so bold right now. And she certainly should be apologizing for lying because that wasn't a good friend. But even after all of this was over, Lana still could never tell Abby the full truth. That thought really hit her hard because she never kept anything from Abby.

Now Lana's only sounding board was her enemy-turned-lover, her current fiancé who would ultimately become her ex. The man wore too many hats in her life to not be involved permanently, but that had been the agreement and she wouldn't be the one to break that deal.

"Is it silly that I'm more excited for your engagement party than I was my own?" Abby asked with a soft laugh. "Don't get me wrong, I love my husband, but I'm just so excited for you and Carson."

Another niggle of guilt hit Lana when she realized she'd have to tell her sister-in-law next week that this epic engagement would officially be called off. She hoped Abby understood that she was only trying to live up to her legacy and continue to grow the women's aspect of the club.

All too soon, everything would go back to being as it was before.

Only everything had changed and nobody outside of her and Carson would fully be able to grasp that concept. Even when they called things off, they would still have this bond they'd formed and Lana didn't know if anything, not even time or distance, could sever that.

Fifteen

Carson pulled into the ranch, the first time he'd been back since the dinner with his dad a few weeks ago. He'd been dodging his calls, not on purpose, but Carson had actually been busy each time his father had called. They'd texted, but there was still that rift between them that had started the second his father had found out about the engagement.

He'd stopped by to see his great-grandfather earlier, but had only stayed a minute. Harmon had looked tired and Carson wanted to let him rest. He'd check back in before the engagement party on Saturday.

Carson couldn't believe the month was nearly

over. His time with Lana would be over in a few short days. At first this entire idea of pretending to be engaged had been preposterous and a month seemed like a lifetime, but now that he was staring down the end, he wasn't in such a hurry to see it all go.

How could either of them go back to how they were before? Nothing between them was the same. They'd forged a unique connection that only the two of them could understand and appreciate because nobody else knew of this ruse. This was something he and Lana would share forever, no matter what happened between them or who they ultimately ended up with.

The idea of another man in her life didn't sit well with Carson. An image of her laughing or sharing her secrets with another seemed so wrong. No way in hell did he want her sharing her bed with some other guy.

On the flip side of all of that, he wasn't so sure any woman would compare to Lana. He didn't know how he would ever get her far enough to the back of his mind in order to fully move on.

Because somewhere along the way, this whole ordeal went from being fake to feeling all too real, and he had no idea what the hell to do with that glaring, realistic fact.

So he'd ignore it. They had an arrangement, one he fully intended to uphold, and telling her his feelings had shifted would make him look like an utter

fool. They'd shifted…so what? He didn't know anything beyond that. He didn't know what he wanted
to do with all of these unwanted emotions. All of
this was completely foreign territory for him.

But the business side? Yeah. That's what he understood, what he knew in his gut was right. So
that's the angle he would continue pursuing. None
of this emotional nonsense that he couldn't quite
explain.

Pushing aside his thoughts, Carson stepped from
his car and realized there was another in the drive.
He'd been so absorbed with his own issues, he'd
totally missed that familiar vehicle.

Sierra Morgan was here. No doubt she was still
trying to uncover the veiled secrets from the diary.
Carson half wondered if it was his own father who
had taken the pages from Arielle's diary, but he still
wasn't sure. There were a limited number of people who would have had the opportunity to sneak
into his house. But no matter who had stolen those
pages, someone Carson trusted had betrayed him
by doing so.

Tamping down the anger, Carson entered his father's home. Voices echoed from the den off the
foyer. Carson stepped through the wide, arched entryway and spotted his father standing against the
bay window, his grandfather, Troy, seated in one of
the leather club chairs, while Sierra sat in another
chair with her notepad and pen.

Carson met his father's gaze. "Is this a bad time?"

Hank shook his head. "Not at all. Sierra just got here. She wanted to interview me about what I know regarding the Wentworth family, as well as Royal's history, since our family has been here since the beginning."

Sierra crossed her legs and smiled at Carson from across the room. "Perfect timing," she said. "Three generations of Wentworths all in one room at my disposal."

Carson respected Sierra and her position—the woman was trying to do her job—but that didn't mean he was in the mood for any Q&A session. He'd come here to talk to his father and try to smooth over any animosity where Lana was concerned.

Which was going to be a moot point in a few days, when he and Lana called off the engagement. But there was something that just irked the hell out of him that his father wouldn't approve of the nuptials.

Damn it. He hated passive-aggressive people and he was doing it to himself with all of these juxtaposing thoughts.

"I was just telling Hank that I'm so excited about the engagement party on Saturday," Sierra added. "That's all anyone around town can talk about."

Just wait until he and Lana broke things off—that would really give people something to talk about.

Carson's eyes shifted to his father, who continued to lean against the window frame.

"It's sure to be a memorable night," Carson stated. "Lana has put a great deal of work into making everything perfect."

"She's a hardworking woman," Sierra agreed. "So do you care to answer some of my questions? I've got so many puzzle pieces that don't fit."

If he fled now he'd look like he was afraid, and nothing ever scared Carson...save for these jumbled-up emotions he couldn't quite get a hold of.

Before he could answer, Tate stepped into the room.

"Oh, I didn't realize we had company."

The teen started to turn, but Sierra called him back.

"I'd love for you to stay," she told him. "I'd be interested in getting your opinion as well."

Tate looked as uncomfortable as Carson felt, but Carson was at least older and more experienced in controlling his outward emotions.

When Tate's eyes landed on Carson, his stepbrother ultimately made his way into the room and took a seat on the leather sofa next to Carson.

"I don't want to keep you all here longer than necessary," Sierra began. "I know you're all busy men and this was a long time ago, but I'd like to discuss Violetta Ford. Her name appears in Arielle's diary. She fascinates me. I'd love to know more about her life. Does anyone know why she disappeared right after she was denied clubhouse membership?"

Carson's grandfather, Troy, scoffed and shook his head. "We have no clue. That's not something we were ever privy to. But she was probably pissed off."

"As far as Violetta, I don't know much about her," Hank admitted.

Sierra pursed her lips. "Okay. Back to your family. How about the breakup between Eloisa Langley and Dean Wentworth?"

Hank raked his hand over the back of his neck. "Listen, we don't want to be rude, but as you said, we are busy. These are questions we simply cannot answer."

"Can't or won't?" she pressed.

Tension fell over the room and Carson had a sinking feeling he was about to play referee or some sort of calming middleman. Sierra was a no-nonsense reporter, and even though she'd come to really embrace the community, she was still hell-bent on doing her job. But Carson knew his grandfather and father weren't about to sit here and pull their family's name through any more scandal than necessary.

What mattered at the end of the day was Harmon. He wanted the century-old feud buried and in order to do that, the secrets needed to come out.

Keeping everything hidden and buried was no way to move forward with a clean slate.

Not only that, but Harmon might also keep his funds from the club if there was any hint that the fighting hadn't stopped once and for all.

Not to mention, Carson and Lana were on the same page in thinking it was time for both families to move on and live at peace here in Royal.

"I think we can trust Sierra with what we know," Carson stated. "She's not here out of any malicious intent. She's been in town long enough to know all the key players and the scandals that have shaped us. I believe her pursuing the truth is going to be the best thing for Royal, not to mention the Langleys and the Wentworths."

Hank's silver eyebrows rose in shock. Troy let out a deep sigh as his focus shifted from Carson back to Sierra.

"And for Harmon's birth mother, I heard rumors she had been in Royal for a little while, then there was a scandal surrounding her and she fled," Hank went on. "We don't know her name."

Sierra's pen moved in a flurry across her notepad and for the first time, Carson also noticed a tiny, old-school tape recorder on the table before her. This reporter covered all her bases.

"So where was Harmon left as a baby?" she asked, glancing back to Hank. "That location might help us figure out some tie to the woman who left him there."

"He was left on the doorstep of his father, Dean Wentworth," Hank told her. "The story goes that he had been in love with Eloisa Langley and was set on marrying her, but something happened and she broke things off. He had some flings and the next thing he knew, a baby showed up, but no mother."

"Dean would never discuss it, and we knew better than to ask," Carson's grandfather added.

Carson listened, soaking up each word, and he was starting to feel a twinge of remorse for Dean Wentworth. Carson was well aware what it was like to fall under the spell of a Langley woman. He knew exactly what that was like, to want to be with someone and…

No, that's not right. He and Dean had nothing in common. Dean actually loved Eloisa, right? Carson didn't love Lana. He valued her, he appreciated her, he enjoyed their time together, but there was no way in hell he could love her. That wasn't in the cards for either of them.

"Once Dean was left with a baby and no mother, he was shunned by the family for a while," Carson's grandfather went on. "After several years, people came around. A baby will do that to people, I guess. But Dean never got over losing Eloisa and Dean had a black mark associated with his name. The mess and feud spawned from there and still carries on to this day."

"Well, that will soon come to an end." Sierra smiled and glanced to Carson. "You have to feel a little pressure, but a whole lot of relief knowing you're obliterating this rivalry started so long ago."

Pressure, yes. Relief…not so much. He wasn't relieved about lying to his family or deceiving anyone and he certainly wasn't relieved about letting Lana go. That actually bothered him more than anything, which was so odd. Since when had she moved to the top slot of priorities in his life?

"Lana and I are both glad we can be the couple to help put this fighting aside and pave the way for the next generation," Carson answered.

At least that was honest. He was glad this all would come to an end between the families. Just because he and Lana weren't going to be married didn't mean that in the future, the families couldn't be civil and cordial toward each other. Royal was a small town with big-city vibes and it was well past time.

"Well, thank you all for sharing your family's history with me," Sierra announced. "The diary pieces are starting to fall into place."

Carson pulled in a deep breath and stretched his arm along the back of the sofa. "Interestingly enough, I discovered Arielle's diary in my bedroom with pages missing."

"What?"

"Are you serious?"

Carson's grandfather and father spoke up at the same time. He tried to gauge their reactions, wondering if either of them had gone into his house and taken those pages.

"Oh, I'm very serious," Carson stated. "Something was on those pages that someone didn't want people to see. Which really makes no sense because I've already read through the diary and so has Sierra. What was so important that pages had to be ripped out?"

Sierra's wide eyes mimicked exactly how he felt. This was absolutely absurd and something he didn't have the time or mental capacity for. He just wanted to get through this engagement party, figure out how to gently call off the engagement, and make the best use of the inheritance the club would be getting from Harmon.

"So you're saying someone came into your house and tore out pages?" Sierra asked. "Who would do such a thing?"

Carson shrugged. "I have no clue, but it would have to be a limited number of family members. No one else had access to my house. I'm so sorry, Sierra. I know Eve loaned it to me in good faith. I'll apologize to her."

"That is so strange," Sierra murmured. "I'm sure the pages will turn up or someone will fess up."

Carson didn't care so much about the missing pages as he did the reason why someone felt the need to sneak into his home and steal.

"I hear there's a surprise to be announced at the engagement party." Sierra wiggled her eyebrows and smiled, clearly ready to move on. "Any chance you want to give me an exclusive?"

Carson shook his head. "I'd like to keep the announcement a surprise."

Sierra nodded. "I can understand that, but I had to try."

She went on to ask several more questions and Tate even joined the conversation when prompted. Finally, Sierra seemed satisfied with her interview and gathered her things.

"This has just been a real pleasure," she told them as she went around the room and shook each man's hand. "The public has been so fascinated with all of my findings in Royal and I just know they are going to eat up this engagement party, the mysterious surprise, and all of this backstory with Harmon's birth mother. That whole misplaced baby is strangely familiar to everything going on now."

"They always say history repeats itself," Carson's grandfather added. "Thank you for stopping by. We'll be seeing you this Saturday at the party."

Once Troy had shown Sierra out, the men were left in the den and Carson got to his feet. He shoved his hands in his pockets and waited until his grand-father came back in.

"Do any of you want to tell me why you took those pages?" he asked, his attention shifting between his father and grandfather.

Both men scoffed, but his grandfather spoke up first.

"Boy, I've never stolen a damn thing in my life so don't start accusing me now."

Carson believed him, so he nodded and showed respect. "My apologies, but you have to understand where I'm coming from. I don't take kindly to someone I trust just taking something from my house without my permission."

He shifted his focus to his father, who remained silent. Carson merely raised his eyebrows.

"What?" his father asked. "You think I did it? Why would I? If I wanted the diary, I would have just told you."

"You're the one upset about this wedding because you've been ingrained to hate the Langleys," Carson growled. "Maybe you took something from the diary that you think would hurt our family name. I don't know. You tell me."

Hank's lips thinned. "There's nothing to tell, so take your accusations and get out."

So much for smoothing things over.

Carson sighed and turned to Tate. "I'll see you Saturday."

Tate merely nodded and remained silent, likely afraid to get involved in this drama. Smart kid. Hopefully by the time he got older and had a little more gumption to stand up for himself, he'd be able to hold his own and choose who the hell he wanted to be with for the rest of his life.

Granted, Carson didn't plan on being with Lana his entire life, but somehow in the last month, his mind had started believing his own lies.

Carson let himself out of the estate and headed to his SUV.

He hadn't seen Lana since last night and he was starting to get cranky. Who knew that faking a relationship could mess with his mind so much?

With the party closing in on them, Carson knew he needed to really make these last days count, because once they had the funds secured, there would be no reason to continue his relationship—fake or otherwise—with Lana Langley.

Sixteen

Lana took Carson's hand as he assisted her from the car. A jumble of nerves curled all through her as she was just steps away from her engagement party.

"You look absolutely stunning," he murmured as he leaned in close. "Green is my favorite color."

She smiled and rested her hand against his freshly shaved cheek. "I remembered and that's why I wore this dress."

The way his warm breath tickled her cheek had her ready to hop back into his car and head back to his house, or hers, she didn't care. She wanted more time alone—she didn't want this to come to an end. She didn't want to go inside that ballroom and smile and lie to everyone she cared about.

But more than anything else, she didn't want to admit that she'd fallen in love with Carson. That was certainly never part of this plan.

"You look like you're ready to run," he joked, easing back to study her face.

Lana stared up into those emerald eyes she'd come to love. Funny how that word bounced around so freely inside her mind, but she couldn't even fathom saying it out loud. Carson would think she'd just gotten caught up in the whirlwind of events, but she knew her feelings for him had changed drastically. She'd gotten to know the real Carson, not the one she'd always been told to hate.

"I'm nervous," she admitted.

"You? I didn't think anything scared you."

Losing him forever scared her in a way she'd never imagined possible. But he wasn't technically hers to lose, which made this entire situation that much more complex and painful. She simply couldn't tell him the full truth of her feelings just yet…and she didn't know if she ever could.

"You know I'm not good at lying," she reminded him. "I just can't stand the thought of going in there and spending hours schmoozing and pretending we're in love."

Okay, well, there would be no pretending on her end.

"You'll do great," he assured her. "We're almost

done and then we'll both get what we want. Don't lose sight of that."

Right. Their goal hinged on this business arrangement, not on her unexpected emotions.

"Ready?" he asked, giving her hand a gentle squeeze.

"Just stay close," she told him. "I need your support."

He blinked, as if shocked by her admission.

"You'll always have my support, Lana," he assured her. "Even after tonight."

She wanted to say something more, but words failed her and Carson turned, urging her with him as he held on to her hand. He led her across the lot and toward the main entrance to the clubhouse and the moment was lost. If she was ever going to confess how she felt, that would have been the time.

So perhaps it was for the best that she didn't say anything. She couldn't risk losing Harmon's very generous funding, but she also didn't want to see any of this come to an end.

Lana stopped, giving a tug on Carson for him to wait.

"Come home with me tonight."

Carson glanced over his shoulder, then slowly turned to face her. "What?"

Nerves were getting the best of her and if she wasn't careful, she'd end up losing that strong control she'd had on this arrangement…and she'd end up with a broken heart.

"I know we're supposed to be slowing down and ending things soon, but I'm not ready yet. Just… stay tonight."

His lids lowered as he closed the minuscule gap between them. Carson framed her face and slid his lips over hers, his touch feathering and arousing, yet so gentle.

"I hadn't planned on being anywhere else tonight," he whispered.

Oh, she was in trouble. More trouble than she'd realized and she didn't know how long she could keep her feelings bottled up inside.

As they reached the entryway, Hank and Harmon were coming up the ramp. Lana hadn't realized Harmon would be here in person.

"There's the happy couple." Harmon held on to the rail as he made his way slowly toward the door. "This is a monumental evening."

"It's so good to see you here," Carson stated, releasing her hand to assist his great-grandfather. "I had no clue you'd be showing up or if you'd feel up to it."

Harmon smiled. "After all this time, you think I'd miss the night we celebrate joining two families? Nothing short of death would keep me away."

Lana went ahead and held the door open for the men, and once Hank took Harmon's hand and led him forward, Carson rested his hand on the small of her back and ushered her inside.

She'd worn an emerald halter with a very low back and a long skirt with a slit—perfectly comfortable, yet enough to hopefully drive Carson mad with need.

As soon as they hit the entryway to the ballroom, Lana nearly choked up on her emotions. All the people mingling already, the green decor accented in gold, the music, the laughter... This was all for her and Carson.

Tears threatened and Lana closed her eyes for a moment. What was wrong with her? She didn't get worked up like this over anything. She hadn't cried over losing the TCC presidency and she'd desperately wanted that title.

But losing the title of Carson Wentworth's fiancée was something else entirely. This was so much more personal, so much more heartbreaking.

And that was the crux of everything that had culminated in this moment. She'd gone and let her heart get involved when she'd sworn not to let that happen.

The DJ spotted them and cut the music, making an announcement about the couple. Everyone broke in to cheers and claps, with a few whistles and yells.

Carson waved and laughed and she had no clue how he was so casual, so...okay with this. They'd worked toward this moment for the last month, but now that it was here, she wasn't feeling as confident as she had been.

"Thank you all for coming," Carson said as the cheers died down. "Lana and I are thrilled everyone is here to support this new chapter in our lives. We hope you enjoy yourselves all evening and stick around for a special announcement later."

The crowd cheered again and Lana could only smile. She hoped nobody could read her stiff body language or her forced grin. Since when did she stand by her man and say nothing at all? That wasn't her personality and she wondered where she'd changed along the way.

Granted, if this had been a real engagement party, she'd be all over making her own announcement and much more comfortable with the atmosphere.

Before her mind could keep winding down that path of unwanted thoughts, various guests started showering her and Carson with love. So many hugs and smiles, so many people genuinely happy for this union.

The DJ made another announcement for a special dance with the happy couple to start off the evening. Carson led her to the dance floor and embraced her as they swayed to a song she hadn't chosen.

"This isn't the song I picked," she muttered.

"No, I did," he told her, staring down into her eyes. "You were doing everything for this and I wanted to pick a song that reminded us of our time together. Do you like it?"

She loved the song, but she actually loved more that he had taken the initiative to change what she'd chosen. He'd actually put some thought into this moment. Did that mean he cared more than he was willing to admit? Did he see her as more than a bargaining tool to get the funds for the club?

On one hand, Lana wished she knew exactly how he felt and what he was thinking where they were concerned, but on the other hand...

Yeah, maybe it was best that she didn't know. If he told her everything between them over the last month had only been to pass the time, she would be even more crushed. Better to walk away with her head high than to be ashamed and even more broken.

She rested one hand on Carson's shoulder and the other in his hand as they swayed to the music. Lana blocked out all the people staring and concentrated on the man holding her.

"We've never danced before," she commented. "This is nice."

"Do you like to dance?" he asked.

She stared into those green eyes and found herself slipping even more. "With the right partner."

"Am I the right partner, Lana?"

She nearly tripped, but thankfully he had a

strong, firm hold on her. He wasn't asking about the dance, and she hadn't been, either.

But Lana didn't respond. Anything she said would give away her true feelings and this was not the place.

The irony of not being able to tell her fake fiancé at their engagement party that she loved him was not lost on her.

Once the song ended, the crowd cheered once again and the DJ pumped up the music to something more upbeat. Lana needed a minute to herself—she needed to regroup and take a breather. For some reason, being intimate with Carson had been easy, and it was the dancing, the hand-holding, the intense stare, and soft words that were really starting to mess with her head.

"I'll be right back," she told him.

He looked like he wanted to say something, but Tate stepped up to them right at that moment.

"Can I talk to Carson?" he asked.

Lana nodded. "Take your time."

Despite Carson's worried look, Lana excused herself and made her way out of the ballroom and toward her office, where she could lock the door for just a moment. If she didn't get control of herself, their ruse would be up and they could kiss the inheritance goodbye.

Why did there have to be such a fine line between love and money?

* * *

"What's up?" Carson asked Tate as his brother pulled him toward the back of the ballroom.

Something had upset Lana and he wanted nothing more than to go after her, but he knew she needed a minute and there was obviously something on Tate's mind.

Carson was going to have to seriously focus on what Tate wanted to talk about, because all he could think of was how perfect Lana had felt in his arms. This night might be all about the sham they'd created, but for reasons he was scared to admit, everything felt so very real.

"I have a confession," Tate stated, cutting into Carson's thoughts.

Carson shifted, his back to the ballroom, and really tuned in to his brother. "What's wrong? And was it illegal?"

Tate glanced away, clearly not impressed with Carson's joke. Something was definitely wrong for his brother to look so solemn.

"Hey, whatever it is, we can get through it," Carson assured him. "Is your girlfriend pregnant?"

Tate jerked. "What? No. It's…the diary."

"What about it?"

Tate squared his shoulders and pulled in a deep breath. "I took those pages."

"What? Why would you need them?"

"There's more," he added. "I overheard you and

Lana in your office the other day and I know you've been lying about all of this."

Carson didn't know what he was more frustrated and shocked about—the fact that his brother had stolen from him, or that Tate knew their secret.

"Why didn't you say anything about knowing before now?" Carson asked, crossing his arms over his chest.

Tate shrugged. "I was upset that you were lying about the engagement and I didn't want you to ruin things for the family. So I went to your house when I knew you weren't home. I was going to take the diary, but thought that would look too suspicious, so I just tore two pages out. I didn't think you'd notice."

The music continued on behind him as people laughed and mingled. Yet all the while Carson could not believe what he was hearing.

"What was on those pages that made you take them?" Carson asked.

"I read about Harmon wondering about his birth mother and how he wished his dad had told someone or had written it down. It got me thinking. Maybe he did. I ended up digging around in Grandpa's attic. I found some letters in an old lockbox."

"Are you kidding? I had no idea all of this was going on," Carson admitted, still stunned at this revelation.

"Nobody did, but I couldn't just let all of these

lies keep going. Between the families feuding and then you and Lana lying, this had to come to an end."

Part of Carson was proud of the courageous step Tate had taken, but that didn't trump the sneaky way he went about it.

"So what did you find in the letters?"

Tate glanced around, likely making sure nobody was approaching them, then shifted his focus back to Carson.

"Dean Wentworth was supposed to marry Eloise Langley."

"Right," Carson said. "But she called it off."

"Yes, but he told everyone he was to blame for it. Eloisa had fallen in love with someone else and asked Dean to say calling off the engagement was his fault. Because he loved her, he did. Then when the baby turned up, which was Harmon, the Langley family, already really hating Dean because they thought he'd cheated on Eloise, had more proof he was no good because he had gotten some unknown woman pregnant."

And thus started a century-long battle between the families. What a mess, all because Dean had been trying to do the right thing on all accounts.

"But that's not all. According to the letters, *Violetta Ford* was Harmon's birth mother," Tate revealed.

"What?" Carson gasped. "No, that can't be right.

She left town after being denied membership into the TCC."

Tate smiled. "It gets better. She never left, never sold her land. She started posing as a male rancher under the guise of Vincent Fenwick. 'Vincent' was the one who bought her land."

Tate paused to catch his breath. Carson could see how excited he was at this discovery.

"When Dean and Eloise ended their relationship, Dean turned to Violetta for comfort and that's when she got pregnant. She couldn't reveal her true identity, so she trusted Dean to raise their child. Can you believe it?"

Carson tried to process everything Tate had said. The truth had been found in an attic by a boy who was invested in this situation far more than Carson knew.

Still, Carson wasn't thrilled about the stolen pages, but in the end, that was nothing if the act revealed the truth once and for all.

"I'm done with lies, Carson. I don't like it and it's done nothing but cause drama and heartache for everyone for years." Tate glanced to his boots, then back up. "And because I think you and Lana really love each other."

Carson was taken aback. "Excuse me?" He couldn't help but laugh at this absurdity. "And where do you get that from? You don't know what's going on between Lana and me."

"Maybe I don't, but when I said I was sick of all the lying, I meant it," Tate went on. "I see the way you guys are with each other. Maybe you're actually meant to be together."

That was just crazy. Carson wasn't about to take relationship advice from a teenage kid. No matter how close he and Tate were, this was Carson's life.

"I'm not discussing this here," Carson stated between clenched teeth. "But we will talk later about privacy. And for someone who doesn't like lying, you've done a good bit yourself."

Tate shook his head. "Listen, I did everything to help put an end to all of this drama. I wouldn't have made a move had I not overheard you and Lana talking."

Carson rested his hand on the back of his neck and rolled around all the information he'd just been handed. Despite the fact Tate took the pages, that he'd known about the fake engagement and kept it to himself, none of that shook Carson more than what Tate thought he saw when he looked at Lana and Carson together. Was there something more than Carson was ready to admit?

All he knew was that he didn't want to delve into anything new where his emotions were concerned. He and Lana had a deal and he didn't intend on going back on his word of letting her go once their commitment was fulfilled.

"Everything okay here?"

Carson turned to see Harmon standing there. Carson opened his mouth to speak, but Tate beat him to it.

"Everything is fine. How are you feeling? Do you want me to get you a seat?"

Harmon waved his wrinkled hand through the air, blowing off the gesture. "Nah, I'm fine, son. It feels good to be out, enjoying life again here at the clubhouse."

"You look really good," Carson told him. "We should break you out more often."

Should he tell Harmon what Tate had discovered? No, tomorrow was soon enough. He'd let Harmon enjoy the party.

Harmon laughed. "I don't know if I have the energy for all of that, but tonight is nice. I never thought this would happen and to know it took a hundred years for the families to join back together, it's just a real dream come true."

Tate's eyes met Carson's and that guilt he'd tried to ignore over the past month came bubbling up with a vengeance. Tate was tired of the lies and maybe Carson should consider taking a chapter from his little brother's book and come clean with absolutely everything.

Seventeen

The knock on her office door had Lana jerking her attention toward the closed door. There was only one person who would come after her.

She pulled in a deep breath and crossed the room, flicked the lock, and twisted the knob. As soon as the door opened, Carson met her gaze with those deep green eyes.

"Are you hiding?" he asked as he stepped in and closed the distance between them.

Lana shrugged. "Maybe for a minute or two."

He rested his hands on her shoulders and rested his forehead against hers. "I don't want to be out there without you."

Lana eased back, surprised by his admission.

She slid her hands up around his neck, threading her fingers through his hair.

"Tate knows," he added.

"Knows what?"

"The truth about us."

Shocked, Lana stilled. "How?"

"He claims he overheard us in my office last week," Carson explained. "He also said he's done with all the lying and he thinks..."

Lana waited for him to finish, but he closed his eyes and seemed to be waging some internal battle with himself.

"Carson."

His lids lifted slowly as he refocused on her. "I need to tell Harmon the truth."

"What? Why? We've worked so hard to make sure we secured this money for the club."

All of this hard work would be for nothing. She hadn't gone through all of this just to end up with no funds for her women's wing and a broken heart. She had to have something good come from these lies and all the manipulation.

"Tate got me thinking when he said he was over the lies," Carson went on. "He also said he thinks you and I are meant to be together."

Lana's breath caught in her throat. But she didn't know where Carson stood, so she tried to blow that off.

"He's a teenager. He hasn't had enough life lessons to come to this conclusion."

Carson shook his head. "Probably not, but he still got me thinking. I need to tell my great-grandfather the truth. I'll find out a way to still get your women's wing. I won't take that from you, but I need to be honest."

Lana waited for him to say something about them. She wanted for him to add in something more, aside from their business agreement. But he didn't.

And that wasn't all she noticed missing from this conversation. She wanted Carson to open up about his feelings for her. If he was done with all the lying, wasn't he referring to everything? She'd never pegged him as a man like her father, but if he couldn't admit there was something more here, then maybe she didn't know him like she thought.

"I'll stand behind whatever you think is best," she finally told him, her heart breaking just a bit more. "If you think Harmon will understand. But I do want him to understand you and I are still friends, that we can make sure the families are merging together from here on out. We can do that without a wedding, right?"

Something came over his face, his lids lowered slightly and his lips thinned. Lana didn't know what he was thinking or feeling or if he planned on letting her in on any of his thoughts.

"Let's wait until after the party," he told her. "He's so happy to be here tonight and everyone is here."

Lana nodded. "I agree. Let's go out and have a good night. We can worry about all the rest to-morrow."

Carson's eyes dropped to her lips. "You're one amazing woman, do you know that?"

She couldn't help but smile. "I'm aware of how awesome I am, but I think you're pretty great, too. That love for your family is pretty amazing."

He slid his lips over hers and everything shifted. There was something in that kiss that seemed... different. But she couldn't quite put her finger on what was happening. They weren't engaged, they weren't even going to pretend after tonight, yet she felt closer and stronger with him than ever.

So what did that mean and how was she going to handle this new chapter when he couldn't even admit how he truly felt?

Carson had planned on talking to Harmon today, but his great-grandfather had called and pretty much demanded Carson meet him at the assisted-living facility.

So Carson stood outside the door to the room and wondered why Harmon was so adamant about this meeting. Regardless of what he wanted, Carson promised Lana he'd come clean today.

He'd spent the night again at her house, and it really should have been the last one, but he wasn't ready to tell her goodbye. He wasn't ready to cut those ties and go back to just being acquaintances.

But that was something he'd have to discuss with her later—right now he had other business to tend to first.

Carson let himself into the suite and closed the door behind him. Across the spacious room, Harmon sat in his chair next to the window. He had a cup of coffee on the table and the local news channel on his television. As soon as he saw Carson, he pointed the remote to the TV and clicked off his program.

"Good morning," Harmon greeted. "Are you alone today?"

Carson stepped into the living area and sank down onto the love seat. "I am. Your call sounded urgent so I came straight here."

Harmon reached for his coffee mug and took a sip, clearly not in a hurry to get this conversation going…which made Carson a bit nervous.

"That party last night was a big hit," he began, turning his attention to Carson. "The crowd seemed to love you and Lana together and they were even more excited about the funds coming to the club for even more renovations and amenities."

Carson had to admit that Harmon's funds would push Cattleman's into something even grander and greater. Every generation always wanted to take the club into a new direction and all eyes were on

Carson now that he was the new president and they had an exorbitant amount of funds.

"Lana seemed upset a bit last night," he added. "I saw you go toward her office."

Carson relaxed further on the sofa and stretched his arm across the back. "She's nervous about this whole process," he admitted.

Harmon's eyes met Carson's. "And what process is that, exactly? Would that be the fake engagement or that you two are actually in love?"

Carson stilled. "Excuse me?"

He knew? Not only did his great-grandfather know about the ruse and the lies, but he also seemed to think Carson and Lana were in love.

That made him the second person to point that out in the span of about twelve hours.

Harmon smiled, the gesture deepening the wrinkles around his eyes and mouth. "I'm no fool, Carson. The two of you went from enemies and at each other during the campaign, to engaged in the span of, what, a few weeks? Besides, I overheard you talking in her office while I was trying to find a quiet corner to catch my breath. So I know everything."

Damn it. He'd been so focused on making sure Lana was okay, plus he was reeling from the bomb dropped by Tate, that he hadn't even noticed anyone else in the hallway.

"I was going to tell you," Carson admitted. "That's what Lana and I were discussing last night.

She's having a difficult time lying and I started having a change of heart as well."

Harmon nodded. "I overheard everything. I'm well aware of your intentions."

"I fully intend to fund the project Lana wants," Carson went on. "I can reconfigure the budget for her. We don't feel right about taking your money when there will be no marriage."

Harmon's bushy white eyebrows drew together. "No marriage? Why the hell not?"

Confused, Carson leaned forward. "You said you knew the truth, that this was all a sham. So the engagement wasn't authentic."

"Maybe not," Harmon agreed. "But just because this started out as a hoax, doesn't mean you two didn't get closer. Am I right?"

Well, yeah, he was right, but could Carson admit such a thing? If he said the words out loud, that would take everything from hypothetical to realistic in a flash.

"Listen."

Harmon winced as he adjusted himself in his chair.

"Are you okay?" Carson asked, starting to stand.

"I'm fine, relax," he insisted. "I'm old and my joints are cranky sometimes. But we're focusing on you and Ms. Langley right now."

Carson didn't like that his great-grandfather was getting older and that he wouldn't be around forever.

Harmon Wentworth wasn't just a staple in Royal, he was in the Cattleman's Club as well.

And he had always been a solid part of Carson's life. He valued what Harmon had to say and had always looked for his opinion on matters.

This was no different, but Carson just didn't know if he was ready to hear all of this.

"As I was saying," Harmon went on. "What I overheard made me so damn proud of you."

Confused, Carson asked, "Proud? I lied to you. We lied to everyone around us."

"You did," Harmon agreed, then shrugged. "But you two overcame your differences and came together. You were putting others' needs first, whether you realize that or not. You put my needs and the needs of the club members first. Not only that, you also realized that what you did wasn't right and you were ready to come clean and confess. All of that makes me realize what a fine man you are and I'm proud you're a Wentworth."

Carson couldn't believe what the man was saying. Out of everything that his great-grandfather would have mentioned, the word *proud* never crossed Carson's mind.

"I still plan on funding the clubhouse."

Another wave of shock overcame Carson. "You do?"

Harmon's smile widened. "Of course. I love that club and I love you. As the president, I want to do everything I can to help you out. Besides, I know the Langley-Wentworth feud is coming to an end."

"How are you so sure of that?"

"It's simple, really. You and Lana will end up together. Maybe not right now—you'll probably be stubborn like us Wentworth men can be, you'll let her go thinking it's for the best. But you won't be able to deny your feelings much longer."

Carson took in all the advice, all the *truth* being handed out freely. Wasn't truth the whole theme as of late? This whole sham started on a misunderstanding that had quickly flipped into a lie. Carson had pulled Lana right along with him.

He'd taken his sworn enemy and pulled her into his drama, and she'd agreed when she could have easily told him no and found other ways to get what she wanted for the club. Never once had he asked her how this whole situation affected her or how she felt. He assumed she was just fine, riding the wave of deceit right along with him.

Carson suddenly realized that Lana wasn't his enemy whatsoever. No, his enemy in all of this was her discomfort and all of the lies. Lana was his...

Everything.

He shifted his gaze back to his still smiling great-grandfather. No, Carson wasn't ready to admit anything, not to Harmon or anyone else. Not until he spoke with Lana and told her everything. Above anyone, she deserved to know where his head was and she deserved to have her own say-so with all of this.

They had something, that much he knew. But did their bond go beyond the loyalties to each other during this temporary process, or was there more... something they could actually build on.

"I appreciate you wanting to tell me the truth," Harmon stated after a bit. "I know your heart is in the right place and I know you will do right by Lana. I'm comfortable with giving up the funds for the club. I want to see it go to the proper place before I pass."

Relief washed over Carson and he couldn't help but smile back. "I need to tell you something else. Tate is the one who stole pages from the diary."

Harmon's eyebrows rose. "Is that right? Why did he do that?"

"He was done with the lies and the animosity between the families," Carson explained. "He didn't want that in place as he got older and he just wanted to smooth things over."

"Another strong Wentworth man."

"That he is," Carson agreed. "The diary gave him a clue that we'd all missed. He found a lockbox with some of Dean's letters up in the attic of the estate."

Harmon shifted in his seat, focusing more on Carson. "A lockbox? I recall my dad having one a long time ago. Forgot where I put the thing. Letters from my dad were in there?"

Carson nodded. "That's what Tate found. The letters fully explained how the feud started."

Carson gave Harmon a brief summary of what Tate told him. He took a deep breath before continuing.

"Harmon, the letters also say that Violetta Ford was your birth mother."

Silence filled the room and Carson wondered if this was too shocking. As much as Harmon was in good health for his age, he was still one hundred years old and his mind wasn't what it used to be.

"Violetta," Harmon whispered. "She was my biological mother? But she left town."

"Violetta was an amazing woman. In the letters it says after Dean and Eloisa broke up, Dean turned to Violetta. But friendship turned to more. After the brief affair she discovered she was pregnant. But here's the shocker—Violetta didn't leave Royal after being denied membership into the TCC. She transformed herself into Vincent Fenwick and continued to run the ranch. She knew Dean would take wonderful care of you, so she dropped you off on his doorstep."

Harmon blew out a sigh. "It's crazy," he muttered. "But in an odd way it makes sense. My dad used to tell me what a great rancher Violetta was, and how she sold her land to an equally great rancher, Vincent Fenwick. Wow, this will take a bit of time to sink in."

Carson was glad Harmon finally got some answers. Carson didn't know a more loyal family than his own and they'd be there to help Harmon adjust to this revelation. The Wentworths might bicker now and then, but they all always had each other's backs. Carson knew at any time his family would do anything for him.

There was someone else who would do anything for him and he was getting more anxious to get back to her. He'd left her bed this morning, wondering where they would go from here. He didn't know if he'd be welcomed back or if they were going to just stop everything once their secret was out.

"Don't you think you should be going?"

His great-grandfather's question pulled Carson from his own thoughts. "Going where?"

"Back to Ms. Langley. You don't want to stay here with me all day. I know your secret, and I'm still donating the funds. There's no reason to keep the inheritance until I pass. I know you and Lana will do what's right for both families and the clubhouse now."

Carson didn't know what to feel at this moment. There was more than relief. There was a sense of calm that overcame him, knowing that for once in his life, he knew exactly what he wanted...who he wanted.

Nothing stood in his way because he wouldn't let it. He wanted to hear what Lana had to say, but he also had quite a bit to tell her as well.

And he was going to start with "I love you."

Eighteen

Lana smoothed her hand over her cream duvet and fluffed her throw pillows into place. She stood back and stared at the perfectly made bed, and all she could think of was how imperfect she and Carson could make it.

When he'd left earlier, she'd lain around and opted to have a lazy Sunday. She'd stayed in bed for a bit, scrolling on social media. So many friends had posted photos from last night and, of course, they'd all tagged her.

When social media became too much, she'd gotten a shower and pulled her hair up in a smooth topknot. She put on her favorite strapless maxi dress that was a vibrant shade of blue. As she stood in her walk-in closet at the island in the middle looking over her earrings, she heard the chime from the security system at the end of her driveway.

She wasn't expecting anyone…unless Carson came back.

They hadn't said much this morning. What was there to say? He'd told her he was going to see Harmon and he would come clean with everything they'd been doing over the past month. Perhaps he was coming back to tell her how the meeting went.

She shouldn't be nervous, but she was. This past month she knew where she stood with Carson. She was his business partner, fake fiancée, and temporary lover. Things were as simple and as complicated as that.

Padding barefoot through her room, she went down the hallway toward her staircase. As she reached the top landing, her front door opened.

Lana stared down into the foyer as Carson stepped inside. His eyes immediately went up, meeting hers and holding her in place.

"I need to get that spare key back," she murmured.

Should her heart flutter like a teenage girl with her first crush? Shouldn't she be over the intensity of his stare by now? The man caused too many strong emotions within her, emotions no man had ever stirred up before. So how was she supposed to cut ties?

On the other hand, all of this was built on lies. Everything they had stemmed from a scandal, and nothing was real. They were both so strong-willed, how could they ever make things work in the real world?

She couldn't stand the silence another second, but she remained at the top of the landing as she rested her hand on the banister.

"Did you see Harmon?"

Carson nodded as he closed the door behind him, but he remained still. "He already knew we were faking the engagement."

"What? How?"

"He overheard us last night talking in your office," Carson explained. "He also overheard us discussing coming clean with him and telling the truth. He said he's proud of our honesty."

Stunned, Lana didn't quite know what to say. The ruse was officially over. This was the moment they'd both been working toward for the past month, but now that it was here, she didn't feel thrilled or excited one bit. There was a little piece of her that felt almost broken. Which was absurd, right? They had nothing solid between them other than their end goal of getting the inheritance.

"Is he keeping the money?" she asked.

"No, he's still donating because he said we had good intentions and we planned on doing the right thing."

Well, at least something right came out of all of this. That was the sole intent of the engagement...so why did she still have that empty pit in her stomach?

"He said something else," Carson added.

"What was that?"

Carson started up the steps, and with each one he kept his eyes locked on hers. Lana's heart beat a little fast as Carson slowly closed that gap between them.

When he reached the top of the landing, he placed his hands on her bare shoulders and turned her to face him fully. There was a light in his eyes she hadn't seen before. Perhaps he was relieved the lies were over. Maybe he was glad to be done with all of this so he could move on with his life.

"He said we belong together."

Lana's breath caught in her throat. "No, he didn't."

Carson offered her a wide smile that had her heart doing a flip. "He absolutely did."

"Why would he say something like that?"

Carson's hands slid up over the column of her throat and up to her face. He held her firmly in that gentle grip as he leaned in closer.

"Because we do," he whispered. "You and I, Lana, we're cut from the same cloth. We complement each other in every way."

Panic set in. Those nerves coursing through her only intensified. The risk of making this real would only end in bigger heartache if they failed. Not to mention, last night Carson didn't include his feelings for her when he was laying out his plan of honesty. Shouldn't she just remove herself now to save that pain later down the road?

"We can't be together," she told him. "We would drive each other crazy. You and I both know we want our way all the time. We're so hardheaded and we'd just end up fighting all the time."

"Have we fought any over the past month?" he asked.

"Well, no."

He slid his thumb along her bottom lip, slowly trying to wear her down, and damn it, it was working.

"I don't want this," she told him, knowing her fear was talking.

Now that the possibility stared her in the face, she couldn't help but be terrified.

"You're lying." He had the audacity to laugh. "You always said you were a terrible liar and I see that now. You know you want to be with me."

Lana flattened her hands against his chest. "That's pretty arrogant even for you."

"Not arrogant," he insisted. "Confident. And I'm certain that you're worried this will all fall apart later down the road. Am I right?"

Lana shrugged, closing her eyes because she didn't want to see the future in front of her. Was he her future? Was this even a possibility? He seemed so sure of this relationship. Even Harmon saw something between them, but had he just been seeing the ruse, or something more authentic?

"What if we fail?" she whispered as tears clogged her throat.

"Look at me," he demanded.

Lana opened her eyes. Carson's smile had vanished, and now that stare was more intense than ever.

"You and I have never failed at anything we put our minds to," he told her. "And I've never wanted anything more than this right here. I love you, Lana."

Everything around her stilled, her breath caught in her throat and those tears she'd been willing away started welling up even more.

"You can't say that."

"Oh, I can and I did," he assured her. "I know you feel the same."

"How could you possibly know that?"

He said nothing as he leaned in, grazing his lips across hers. Carson coaxed her lips apart, gently, softly. Lana opened for him. Her hands on his chest curled in, gripping his T-shirt.

Carson slid his hands down to the top of her strapless dress. He continued making love to her mouth as he eased down the fabric, ultimately sending the material into a puddle at her feet.

Suddenly his hands were everywhere on her, removing her bra and panties in a flurry. His actions were hurried, but his touch gentle.

And then he stepped back, staring at her, raking that emerald gaze over her bare body. Not only was she physically stripped bare, but her raw emotions were also on display.

And she was wearing absolutely nothing now but his ring.

"Tell me you love me," he murmured.

There was no more hiding. She might be afraid of everything that could go wrong, but what if everything went right?

"You know I do," she admitted.

Carson smiled, the brightness reaching his eyes and making her heart melt even more.

"There's no more feud between our families," he told her. "We're not living in the past anymore. I want a future, with you, for real this time."

"Wait…you want to marry me?"

Carson laughed. "Did you think I just wanted to keep sleeping with you? Honey, you should know better than that. I'm all in with you. That ring on your finger isn't just a prop anymore. It's real, just like the life I want with you."

Lana refused to deny herself anymore. She'd always gone after what she wanted and tried to live up to Abby's legacy, so maybe it was a good thing she had that fear in her. That strong emotion would only make her want to work even harder at making this work.

"Are you going to stand there or take me back to bed?" she asked with a smile.

"Are you going to marry me?"

Lana wrapped her arms around him and smacked a kiss on his lips. "I wanted to be TCC president, but I can handle being the first lady."

Carson laughed as he lifted her in his arms and carried her to her bedroom. Lana might have had a different idea for her life, but that was nothing compared to the thrilling one she'd just been handed. From now on, she and Carson would be side by side in absolutely everything...and nothing could stop them.

* * * * *

Look for the next book in the
Texas Cattleman's Club: Fathers and Sons series,
Rafe's story

The Rebel's Return
by Nadine Gonzalez

Available next month!

#2857 THE REBEL'S RETURN

Texas Cattleman's Club: Fathers and Sons • by Nadine Gonzalez

Eve Martin has one goal—find her nephew's father—and her unlikely ally is hotelier Rafael Wentworth, who's just returned to Texas and the family who abandoned him. Soon she's falling hard for the playboy in spite of their differences...and their secrets.

#2858 SECRETS OF A BAD REPUTATION

Dynasties: DNA Dilemma • by Joss Wood

Musician Griff O'Hare uses his bad-boy persona to keep others at bay. But when he's booked by straitlaced Kinga Ryder-White for her family's gala, he can't ignore their attraction. Yet as they fall for one another, everything around them falls apart...

#2859 HUSBAND IN NAME ONLY

Gambling Men • by Barbara Dunlop

Everyone believes ambitious Adeline Cambridge and rugged Alaskan politician Joe Breckenridge make a good match. So after one unexpected night and a baby on the way, their families push them into marriage. But will the convenient arrangement withstand the sparks and secrets between them?

#2860 EVER AFTER EXES

Titans of Tech • by Susannah Erwin

Dating app creator Will Taylor makes happily-ever-afters but remains a bachelor after his heart was broken by Finley Smythe. Reunited at a remote resort, they strike an uneasy truce after being stranded together. The attraction's still there even as their complicated past threatens everything...

#2861 ONE NIGHT CONSEQUENCE

Clashing Birthrights • by Yvonne Lindsay

As the widow of his best friend, Stevie Nickerson should be off-limits to CEO Fletcher Richmond, but there's a spark neither can ignore. When he learns she's pregnant, he insists on marriage, but Stevie relishes her independence. Can the two make it work?

#2862 THE WEDDING DARE

Destination Wedding • by Katherine Garbera

After learning a life-shattering secret, entrepreneur Logan Bisset finds solace in the arms of his ex, Quinn Murray. Meeting again at a Nantucket wedding, the heat's still there. But he might lose her again if he can't put the past behind him...

HDCNM0122B

SPECIAL EXCERPT FROM

(H) HARLEQUIN
DESIRE

*Alaskan senator Jessup Outlaw needs an escape...
and he finds just what he needs on his Napa Valley
vacation: actress Paige Novak. What starts as a fling
soon gets serious, but a familiar face from Paige's past
may ruin everything...*

Read on for a sneak peek of
What Happens on Vacation…
by New York Times *bestselling author Brenda Jackson.*

"Hey, aren't you going to join me?" Paige asked, pushing wet hair back from her face and treading water in the center of the pool. "Swimming is on my list of fun things. We might as well kick things off with a bang."

Bang? Why had she said that? Lust immediately took over his senses. Desire beyond madness consumed him. He was determined that by the time they parted ways at the end of the month their sexual needs, wants and desires would be fulfilled and under control.

Quickly removing his shirt, Jess's hands went to his zipper, inched it down and slid the pants, along with his briefs, down his legs. He knew Paige was watching him and he was glad that he was the man she wanted.

"Come here, Paige."

She smiled and shook her head. "If you want me, Jess, you have to come and get me." She then swam to the far end of the pool, away from him.

HDEXP0122B

Oh, so now she wanted to play hard to get? He had no problem going after her. Maybe now was a good time to tell her that not only had he been captain of his dog sled team, but he'd also been captain of his college swim team.

He glided through the water like an Olympic swimmer going after the gold, and it didn't take long to reach her. When she saw him getting close, she laughed and swam to the other side. Without missing a stroke or losing speed, he did a freestyle flip turn and reached out and caught her by the ankles. The capture was swift and the minute he touched her, more desire rammed through him to the point where water couldn't cool him down.

"I got you," he said, pulling her toward him and swimming with her in his arms to the edge of the pool.

When they reached the shallow end, he allowed her to stand, and the minute her feet touched the bottom she circled her arms around his neck. "No, Jess, I got you and I'm ready for you." Then she leaned in and took his mouth.

Don't miss what happens next in...
What Happens on Vacation...
by Brenda Jackson, the next book in her
Westmoreland Legacy: The Outlaws series!

Available March 2022 wherever
Harlequin Desire books and ebooks are sold.

Harlequin.com

HDEXP0122B

Marcus watched as she got to her feet. He was grateful to see that she was steady.

"Can we have a minute?" Marcus asked Blade.

"Yeah. Hang on to her good arm," his friend replied. Then he walked away, taking Dawson with him.

"What?" she asked, offering him a sweet smile.

"I'm going to find who did this. I promise you. And you're going to be okay. Jamie Weathers is the best emergency physician this side of the Colorado River. Hell, this side of the Missouri River. He'll fix you up. But don't leave the hospital until you hear from me. You understand?"

"I got it," she said. "I'm going to be fine. It's all going to be fine. I barely had twenty bucks in my bag. He didn't even get my phone. I had that in my back pocket. Nor my keys. Those were in my hand. So he basically got nothing except the cash and my driver's license."

Things didn't matter. "You want me to let Brian and Morgan know?"

"Oh, God, no. Please don't do that." She looked panicked. "Morgan can't have stress right now. I'm grateful that her room is on the other side of the building. Otherwise, she could be watching this spectacle."

They would want to know. But it was her decision. And she was in pain. "Okay," he said, giving in easily.

"Thank you," she said.

"Go get fixed up. I'll talk to you soon."

She nodded.

"And, Erin…" he added.

"Yeah."

"I'm really glad that you're okay."

Don't miss
Trouble in Blue *by Beverly Long,*
available March 2022 wherever
Harlequin Romantic Suspense
books and ebooks are sold.

Harlequin.com